North American Legends

North American Legends

edited by
VIRGINIA HAVILAND

illustrated by Ann Strugnell

COLLINS
New York and Cleveland

Library of Congress Cataloging in Publication Data
Main entry under title:
North American legends.
  Bibliography: p. 205
  SUMMARY: Presents tall tales indigenous to America, tales of
European and African immigrants, and folklore of American Indians
and Eskimos.
  1. Tales, American. 2. Indians of North America—Legends.
[1. Folklore—United States. 2. Indians of North America—
Legends] I. Haviland, Virginia, 1911-   II. Strugnell, Ann.
▲ JPZ8.1.N795   398.2'0973   78-26999
  ISBN 0-529-05457-4

First United States publication 1979
by William Collins Publishers, Inc.,
New York and Cleveland.

This collection © Virginia Haviland 1979
Illustrations © Faber and Faber Ltd. 1979
Printed in the United States of America

Contents

Acknowledgements

The editor thanks the following for permission to use copyright material:– The author and McIntosh & Otis Inc. for "The Giant Sturgeon" from *The World of Manabozho, Tales of the Chippewa Indians* by Thomas B. Leekley. Copyright © 1965 by Thomas B. Leekley. Reprinted by permission of the Author and McIntosh and Otis, Inc.

Houghton Mifflin Company and Grace J. Penney for "How the Seven Brothers Saved Their Sister" from *Tales of the Cheyennes* by Grace Jackson Penney. Copyright 1953 by Grace Jackson Penney. Reprinted by permission of the author and Houghton Mifflin Company.

Harper & Row Publishers Inc. for "In the Beginning" and "Raven Lets Out the Daylight" from *Raven-Who-Sets-Things-Right* by Fran Martin. Copyright © (text) by Frances McEntee Martin. Reprinted by permission of Harper & Row Publishers Inc.

Bolt and Watson Ltd. and Crane Russak & Co. for "How Coyote Brought Fire" from *Coyote the Trickster* by Gail Robinson and Douglas Hill. Published in Great Britain by Chatto & Windus Ltd. and in the United States in 1976 by Crane Russak & Company, Inc.

Charles E. Tuttle Co. Inc. for "Sedna the Sea Goddess" from *Shadows of the Singing House* by Helen R. Caswell, published by Charles E. Tuttle Co. Inc.

Thomas Y. Crowell Company and Marie Rodell-Frances Collin Literary Agency for "How Saynday Got the Sun" from *Winter-telling Stories* compiled by Alice Marriott. Copyright © 1974 by Alice Marriott. Reprinted by permission of Thomas Y. Crowell

Simon & Schuster Inc. for "Strong but Quirky" from *Yankee Thunder* by Irwin Shapiro.

Coward, McCann & Geoghegan Inc. for "Johnny Appleseed" reprinted by permission of Coward, McCann & Geoghegan Inc. from *Tall Tale America* by Walter Blair. Copyright 1944 by Walter Blair; renewed 1972.

Introduction

This is an anthology of myths, legends, and tales of North America, presented under the broad term "legends", which is used here to mean any stories coming from the past. They have been selected from a large body of folklore that has become an integral part of American literature, falling naturally into four main groups: stories of the American Indians and Eskimos; stories of the Black Americans; tales brought by immigrants from Europe; and indigenous American "tall tales".

Before European settlers arrived in North America an American Indian folklore existed, the creation of a people who observed nature closely and evolved a mythology which explained the origins of the universe and natural phenomena in poetic terms. They believed firmly in supernatural forces, and their legends told of culture heroes and shape-shifters who used magic. Animals had power to turn into people and people into animals. The animal stories, like animal folklore of many other countries, are often humorous, and the characters are accomplished tricksters. In Indian stories, the leading figures of this type, who alternate between doing good and doing evil, are Coyote and Raven, but Badger, Mink and Blue Jay appear as tricksters in stories from certain regions. In African tales Rabbit plays a similar role.

The first attempts to preserve the oral heritage of the Indians were made by government agents working among them, and by traders and missionaries. These were followed by trained anthropologists and ethnologists who viewed folklore scientifically. Folklore scholars have been unhappy about some of the "literary" treatments of Indian mythology in later retellings for the young, which failed to acknowledge sources and prettified the spare, direct stories. Even the eminent Henry Rowe Schoolcraft introduced elaborations into the versions he recorded. But such acknowledged anthropologists and meticulous documenters as Alice Marriott, Maria Leach, Harold Courlander, Richard Chase, and John Bierhorst have made contributions to collections of legends for both children and adults.

A rich variety of tales came to America with immigrants from Europe and Africa, and their stories can be seen to have overlaid Indian lore, especially in the south-eastern parts of the United States and in French Canada. In the eastern states as well as farther west, the folklore of Indians and Blacks became mixed. A clear instance is seen in the Cherokee tale included here, "Big Long Man's Corn Patch". The famous folklorist Stith Thompson shows marked parallels between the two traditions in his *European Tales Among the North American Indians*,[1] while the folklorist Alan Dundes has written in *African Tales Among the North American Indians*[2] about tales shared by Blacks and south-eastern Indian tribes. Thompson considers the animal tales in both traditions to be borrowings from European folklore. Magic from African voodoo also became mixed with the magic of the Indians. The French of Acadian Canada, in the far north, brought their tales to Louisiana in the far south, and there they mixed with the voodoo culture from Africa. The practice of voodoo reached the United States by way of Haiti and was scattered all over the north as well as the south. Sorcerers met annually in Louisiana and used a language called "gumbo", which was a patois of African and French used in the West Indies and Louisiana. Black American tales told widely in Georgia, the Carolinas, and most of all on the Sea Islands lived on there in a kind of cultural isolation.

1. Colorado College, Colorado Springs, Colorado, 1919.
2. *Southern Folklore Quarterly*, v. 29, 1965: 207–219.

English and Scottish settlers brought their tales and ballads to the mountain regions of Southern Appalachia, and later carried some of them to the Ozarks. They kept their stories alive by telling them in social and work gatherings, and the tales and songs acquired a distinctive overlay of mountain Americanisms. Being cut off by natural barriers, these immigrants were little influenced by the more sophisticated world outside, and their folklore changed remarkably little over the years.

In the northern states, German, Scandinavian, Dutch, and Slavic immigrants shared their stories, too. Washington Irving made use of German tales for his Hudson River stories about Rip Van Winkle and Ichabod Crane.

Recorders of Indian folklore began collecting in the later nineteenth century. Appalachian lore was gathered later, in the early 1900s—the songs first and the stories later. Such seekers as storyteller Richard Chase and teachers in rural mountain schools and colleges like Marie Campbell and Leonard Roberts scoured the Appalachian countryside, sometimes locating tellers through their students.

With the conquest of the frontiers, exploration to the west coast, and the rise of the industrial age an entirely indigenous hero came into being. In what has been called the most typical of all American folktales, vigorous American folk heroes developed from historical into popular romantic figures. Tales of their bigger-than-life deeds in the growing nation—clearing the land, taming wild horses, triumphing at sea, working in steel mills and on the railroad—became more and more colorfully exaggerated and humorous with retelling. This "tall tale" is a combination of the credible and the totally impossible, as fantastic as the European stories of Baron Munchausen yet uniquely American. Scholars have rightly questioned the use of the term "folklore" here, since it is recognized that stories about some of the more than two dozen well-known folk heroes celebrated in so-called tall-tale legends were invented by journalists. Such writings have been labeled "fakelore". Paul Bunyan of logging fame was a figure promoted by the lumber industry and his deeds were recounted first in 1914 in an advertising booklet. Some of his exploits, however, arose from oral tradition rather than from such exploitation. The stories were carried westward from logging camps in the great Northern Wood, enriched perhaps by both Scandinavian and Indian lore. Tales legitimately termed "folk" as well as "concocted" evolved about such historical legendary figures or culture heroes as Davy Crockett, Daniel Boone, Kit Carson and Johnny Appleseed. Some heroes achieved special popularity as subjects of ballads, like John Henry, the black riveter who fought a contest with the steam drill on the railroad. Ballads also celebrated Casey Jones of baseball fame and Johnny Appleseed, the New Englander who carried seeds of the apple tree throughout the Midwest.

Sid Fleischman, who has created his own fantastic tall tales, has stated that "It was no accident that the tall tale flourished on the frontier. . . . In laughter, pioneers found a way of accommodating themselves to the agonies that came with the land."[1] James Bowman, a collector of both Pecos Bill and Mike Fink legends "from the annals of the camp fire and the round-up", recognized that in these stories "the frontiersmen freed themselves from the drab cruel world of hardship and tragedy which encompassed them everywhere. One tall tale led to a taller tale".

The Archive of Folksong at the Library of Congress has recordings of thousands of songs and tales collected in the field, and its books and journals also contain stories that were found and set down by early anthropologists and ethnologists who were members of the American Folklore Society and regional folklore societies. Further stories exist in this national library's archives in the manuscripts from the Federal Writers' Project of the Works Progress Administration of the United States Government during the Great Depression.

1. *Horn Book Magazine*, v. 52, Oct. 1976: 470.

INTRODUCTION

Most of the stories are given here just as they were recorded by early collectors: some have been retold later by skillful storytellers and ethnologists; a few have been retold by myself with only minimal changes in style. Regional idioms have been kept where their meaning is clear, to retain the local flavor. There is still some disagreement about the proper way to present folklore: ethnologists and anthropologists have been mainly concerned that the material should be accurately recorded, while storytellers and editors for young people are interested most of all in folklore as literature. But fortunately some ethnologists are able to present their material attractively as well as accurately. I have tried to choose versions which are both true to the origins and enjoyable to read, for an anthology which of course can include only a fraction of the riches of American folklore.

Virginia Haviland

Indian and Eskimo Tales

The Giant Sturgeon

One day Manabozho was sitting beside the fire with his grandmother.

"Nakomis," he asked, "I wonder, are we the only people in the world? I seem to remember that long ago, when I was a very small boy, there was another small boy I played with."

"There was another boy," said the grandmother.

"What was his name?"

"Nahpootee."

"Was he . . . was he my brother?"

"Yes."

Manabozho was silent for a long time, quietly wishing for his brother, remembering faintly the childish fun they had shared when they had played and rolled about together on the wooded trails.

"Was he an older brother, Nakomis?"

"Yes, but you were twins."

"What happened to this brother, grandmother?"

"He was raised by your father's sister for your father."

"Then how was it that he and I played together?"

"Sometimes he was brought to see you, after it was known that I had saved you and that you were alive."

"By speaking you raise many questions, old grandmother," said Manabozho. "But first of all, where is my father?"

"Far away. He is Wabun, the West Wind."

"And my mother?"

"She may have died when you were born. She may be on an island in the lake, living under a spell that the great wendigo* has cast upon her."

"You do not know, grandmother?"

"I do not know."

"But you raised me?"

"Yes, I found you under an old wooden bowl. Five days after you were born I found you."

"Someone left me there to die?"

"It would be kinder to say you were forgotten. Your father's sister took Nahpootee away. Let us say that she forgot you."

"Where is Nahpootee, my older brother, now?"

"A great wendigo has changed him to a . . . to a tree, I think," said Nakomis.

Again Manabozho fell silent. "You have often told me of my father, Nakomis," he observed when next he spoke. "But I know nothing of my mother. You said I had a mother?"

"Of course," replied his grandmother.

"And who was she?"

"I would rather once more tell you of your father, Wabun, the West Wind."

"But I asked you of my mother, not my father."

Old Nakomis sighed. "Your mother was my daughter, a great-granddaughter of the moon," she said.

"Where is my mother now?" asked Manabozho.

"I have told you that I do not know. One story says your

*Sorcerer.

mother died when you were born. I do not know. I was not there. Another story tells of the spell that was cast upon her."

"What about my father? Surely he—"

"He left your mother before you were born. I have had to be a father and a mother to you."

Manabozho made a sour face. "You have had a hard task, grandmother," he observed.

"It has not been easy."

"I shall find my father some day, and I shall punish him for what he brought upon you, and for his cruelty to my mother."

"He will kill you if you find him, Manabozho."

"He will find me hard to kill," said her grandson firmly. He paused a moment. "Grandmother?" he asked.

"What?"

"There must have been others in the world besides my father, my mother, my brother, you, and me. Tell me, am I right? Were there once other people in the world?"

"Yes."

"Tell me of them."

"The great wendigo has turned them all to trees. They are all trees firm-rooted in the soil of a far island on this lake."

"Was this done by the same great wendigo who turned my older brother Nahpootee into a tree?" he asked.

"The same."

"I shall find a way to free them all!" said Manabozho.

Nakomis laughed, almost scornfully. "If you try, it will be a short life you'll have!"

"I shall try, and we shall see! What must I do first, grandmother?"

"You must do nothing first—or ever! Stay here where you are!"

"I shall find my brother, punish my father, avenge my mother, and free all the people. I have told you, Nakomis! Now speak and tell me what is the first thing I must do!"

The grandmother looked up slyly from the moose skin she was sewing, studying her grandson's face for a moment. Then very grimly she went back to work, saying nothing.

Manabozho's voice became insistent. "Tell me, grandmother! Tell me now! I must know!"

Nakomis looked up again and sighed. "You are determined?" she asked.

"Yes."

"The first task is the easiest, though it is so hard that surely you can never do it."

"Tell me what it is, and I shall do it."

"First, you must kill the giant sturgeon."

"Why?"

"You will find the people hungry after you have freed them from the spell."

"Well, what of that?"

"There must be fish in the great lake. When the people are no longer trees, they will need food."

"Again you speak in riddles, grandmother. If I kill the giant sturgeon, how will that put fish in all the lakes?"

"First, Manabozho, you must kill the giant sturgeon. If you do that I will tell you what next there is to do." Nakomis paused. Her old eyes watered. "You cannot kill him, Manabozho. It is far more likely that he will kill you first!"

"Nevertheless," said her grandson, "I am going to try."

Nakomis moved the wigwam down beside the lake to watch Manabozho as he prepared for his encounter.

The young man took down his ax and whetstone and began to sharpen one with the other. "My father, my father," the stone seemed to say as it ground down the ax blade. Manabozho turned his head to listen. "My father, my mother, my father, my mother," the stone repeated as it did its work. Manabozho held his ear down closer. "My

24

father, my brother, my father, my mother," the whetstone continued.

"Yes! Yes! I shall see them all before I finish!" cried Manabozho. "Now I must sharpen my ax and knife to cut lance handles and arrow shafts. First we must kill the giant sturgeon. We must put food in the lake, lest the people starve when we release them from the spell the great wendigo has cast."

When he was through, Manabozho cut a tough, straight shaft of spruce for his lance and split a piece of clear white pine into a dozen arrows, rounding them off carefully with his knife. When he was finished he took his fire drill, weapons, paint, and other war gear, stepped into his canoe, and pushed off with a paddle.

Nakomis stood on the shore, tears rolling down her leathery face.

"Do not grieve, grandmother," called Manabozho, looking backward.

"Your mother and your brother, both are gone. They have vanished in the land of the wendigo. Now you are going, too. I shall not see you any more!"

"Do not fear, grandmother." Manabozho looked toward the prow of his canoe. A little squirrel had jumped in with him and now stood perched upon a thwart, apparently unconcerned about the dangers of the journey. "See, Nakomis!" Manabozho cried. "The squirrel is not afraid! He knows we shall come back, he to his hole within the tree, I to our wigwam here beside the lake!"

His grandmother looked out sorrowfully at the canoe and its two riders. "The squirrel is as big a fool as you!" she said. "The giant sturgeon will kill both of you!"

Manabozho paddled far out into the deepest part of the lake, put a bone hook on a piece of line, dropped it overboard, and began a singsong chant:

"Come, great sturgeon, try my strength, I am Manabozho!"

Deep down in the lake the big fish lay half asleep. Far

above him he heard Manabozho calling him to fight. Rather sleepily he called the sunfish to him.

"Who is that making all the noise above us?" he inquired.

"Manabozho."

"And who is Manabozho?"

"He is a young manitou* who lives on the shore with his grand—"

"Enough!" said the giant sturgeon. "Go up and pull on his hook. Pull it off his line so he won't bother us!"

The sunfish did as he was told. He swam up to where Manabozho's hook lay in the water and gave a sharp tug on it, as if to break the line.

Quickly Manabozho set the hook and pulled his catch into the boat. When he saw the sunfish he was very angry. "What are you doing on my hook, you little dirty fish!" he yelled. "I'll teach you to come when I call the giant sturgeon!" He tore the fish into several small pieces and threw each piece as far as he could from the canoe. Surprisingly, as each fragment hit the water it turned into another sunfish that swam off into the shallows.

"Well!" said Manabozho, quite amazed. "Perhaps this is something Nakomis spoke of. After I have brought the people back to life, they will have lots of sunfish."

Once again he dropped his hook and line overboard and began his chant:

"Come, great sturgeon, try my strength. I am Manabozho!"

This time the great fish made a couple of angry turns around the rocks where he had been resting. He paused, looked up at the canoe, then called the pike over to him.

"Someone up in that canoe says he is Manabozho," said the giant sturgeon angrily. "He wants me to fight him. Did you ever hear of anyone called Manabozho?"

"Oh, yes," said the pike. "He is a young manitou who

*A being with power over the forces of nature.

claims to have great power. He lives with his grandmother in a wigwam over on the lake shore."

"He doesn't interest me," said the giant sturgeon. "Go up and break his line. Get him out of here!"

The pike streaked upward like an arrow, struck the hook viciously, but the line did not break. Instead, he felt his head jerked backward, found himself pulled out of the water, through the air, and landed with a thud in the bottom of the canoe.

"Why are you fouling my hook?" shouted Manabozho angrily. "You look like a snake to me!" He took his ax and stunned the pike with a blow back of the snout, grasped his knife, and cut the fish into a hundred pieces. Each piece he threw as far as he could. As it hit the water it turned into a smaller pike and swam away.

"There!" said Manabozho. "Now I begin to understand. When they return, the people will have pike as well as sunfish!"

In a moment he dropped his hook and line over the side again. Once more he let his little chant ring out defiantly:

"Come, great sturgeon, try my strength. I am Manabozho!"

Now the giant fish lashed about angrily, ground his sharp teeth together, stood on his tail almost upright on the lake bottom, and looked up at Manabozho. This time he called no other fish to him. Instead, he gave a mighty swish with his tail and rushed upward with his mouth wide open, the water churning through it like a whirlpool. He took in Manabozho and his canoe with one gulp, swallowed, and then quietly settled back into the depths to digest the morsel he had eaten.

When Manabozho came back to his senses, everything was dark. He had to think for a moment to recall just where he was. He reached out and touched the side of his canoe; it was familiar. He felt for his paddle and found it; that was reassuring. But then he remembered the open mouth of the sturgeon and knew just where he was. That was a fearful thought!

Out somewhere in the surrounding darkness was a little whirring, chirping sound. And from above him came a deep noise somewhat like the beating of a drum. Manabozho choked back his fear and listened to the sounds about him.

Suddenly he knew what made the chirping noise: it was his little friend the squirrel! They had both been swallowed together. They were inside the giant fish together!

"Squirrel!" he called. "Are you there, little brother?"

"Of course I'm here!" the squirrel retorted. "You don't seem to be doing much to get me out of here! Of course I'm here! Who do you think is making all this noise? I've been trying to wake you for hours! Are you all right?"

Manabozho felt his arms and legs, then moved about in the canoe a little. "I guess I'm all right," he said. "I don't seem to hurt much anywhere."

"Well, then, what are you going to do to get us out of here?"

Manabozho was taken aback. "What can I do?" he asked.

"You might build a fire so we could see a little."

"How can I build a fire?"

"You have your drill, don't you?"

Manabozho felt in the bottom of the canoe and found it. "Yes," he said. "But I have no tinder."

"You have a canoe!" the squirrel retorted. "When you have a canoe, you have birchbark!"

Slowly Manabozho began to strip off shreds of bark to make a pile of tinder. When he knew he had enough he picked up the drill. In the background he heard the continuous, deep-pitched, drumlike, booming noise he had heard when he had regained his senses.

"I wonder what that noise is?" he asked aloud as he began to drill on the block he had set underneath the tinder.

28

"Maybe we can find out when we have a light," the squirrel replied.

In a moment there was a tiny spark down in the tinder. Manabozho cupped it in his hands and blew upon it. All at once there was a little flame. He put on bigger bits of bark, then broke two or three of his new arrows into kindling, and finally split off part of his paddle blade to feed the flame.

At last he dared to take his eyes away from what he was doing and to look overhead. The little fire lit up the inside of his prison with a fitful, flickering glow. He might well have been inside a cave with a wet, shiny ceiling. And just above him was a spot that kept moving up and down in time to the great deep booming noise he heard.

Manabozho lowered his eyes and saw his friend the squirrel still sitting on the thwart at the bow of the canoe. The squirrel, too, was watching the moving spot above their heads.

"I wonder what it is?" he asked, pointing to the place where the prison seemed to be pumping back and forth.

"I don't know," answered Manabozho.

"It might be the giant sturgeon's heart," the squirrel observed.

"Of course it is!" said Manabozho. "That's just what I was thinking! That's why it jumps up and down and makes the booming noise we hear!"

"Now you're really thinking!" the squirrel said. "And perhaps, if you were to strike it with your lance . . ." He let his voice run out as if engaged in thought. "If you were to spear it, we just might . . ."

"Enough!" shouted Manabozho. "That's just what I was going to do!" He raised the weapon and drove it deep into the great fish's heart. The giant sturgeon shuddered, turned convulsively as if in agony, then suddenly was still.

"Now what shall we do?" asked Manabozho.

"He'll float up on top of the water, maybe," said the squirrel.

29

"I know. But how will we get out?"

"You have your ax and lance. Will they help?"

"Of course they will!" said Manabozho.

There was no doubt that the body of the sturgeon was rising through the water. After what seemed a very long time, all upward motion stopped. When Manabozho was certain they were floating on the surface, he rose and drove his lance out into the sunlight. Suddenly, from the air outside, he heard the crying of a hundred gulls.

"Help us, little brothers!" he called to the birds who came flocking about the carcass of the sturgeon. "Help us to come out into the air and sunlight where you are!"

The gulls began to work with their bills from the outside while Manabozho plied his lance and ax from within. Almost at once there was a hole large enough to let the squirrel escape. Then, a few moments later, out came Manabozho, pulling his canoe after him.

He looked about. He might well have been on a small island, smooth and bare and treeless. Across the lake, in the direction toward which the wind was blowing, was Nakomis's wigwam. He could see her standing on the shore line watching for him.

He turned and saw his friends the gulls. One by one they were beginning to fly away.

"Wait!" he called. "I would adorn you for the help you gave me. But first I must do something for the squirrel, my little brother."

Manabozho reached down into the canoe and took out his paints. Very carefully he painted his friend the squirrel a reddish brown along the back and sides, a lighter, flame-colored reddish white beneath.

"There," he said. "Let your color, red squirrel, always remind you of the fire you had me build within the sturgeon."

"There were some other things I put in your mind as well," the red squirrel chattered.

Manabozho grinned. He reached behind the red squirrel

30

and turned his tail straight upwards. He made it big and fluffy. He straightened each hair so that it stood outward. "There," he said. "Carry your tail with pride, little brother, for having brought me both ideas and courage."

Manabozho looked across the water to his grandmother's wigwam. A sharp wind had come up and was driving the body of the great sturgeon toward the shore. The gulls were circling overhead eager to have their reward and to be away.

"Come!" he called to them, picking up his white and blue and gray paints. Quickly, surely, he adorned them. White he made them on the underside, light gray and pale blue above.

"There!" he said when he had finished. "Now when men return from their enchantment and see you, they will ask how you came to be so beautiful. You must tell them that you were adorned by Manabozho for having helped him escape from inside the giant sturgeon."

By now the great hulk of the fish was grating on the lake shore. Nakomis came running down to see what she should do. The gulls soared away above the water. Manabozho took up the red squirrel, set him on dry land, watched him go scampering off into the trees.

Nakomis stood, a great knife in her hand, looking at the sturgeon. Half fearfully, half hopefully, she turned her face to Manabozho. "Have you done enough?" she asked.

"I must set the people free," replied her grandson. "And I must find my brother and punish my father for his cruelty to my mother."

Nakomis sighed. She took her knife and began to strip away the meat. Each piece she cut she threw away. As it struck the water it turned at once into a smaller sturgeon and swam off into the rushes.

"Well," said Manabozho as he watched, "now there will be fish enough for all the people when I bring them back to life."

31

[In another story, "The Fight with the Wendigo", Manabozho frees his brothers and others from the Wendigo's
enchantments, and in "The Fight with Wabun" he finds
and wounds his father, Wabun.]

How the Seven Brothers Saved Their Sister

Long and long ago, there lived among the Cheyennes an old woman and her young granddaughter. They had no other relatives, and lived together in a little lodge, where the grandmother taught the young girl, Red Leaf, to make fine beaded robes and moccasins. Nowhere in all the tribe was there a better robe-maker than Red Leaf.

Now it so happened that not very far from there lived seven brothers. They had no father, no mother, and no sisters. The seven of them lived together, with the youngest, Moksois, staying at home to take care of the camp while the six older brothers went out to hunt.

"Grandmother," said Red Leaf, one day, "I would like to have Moksois and his brothers to be my brothers. They are great hunters, and could bring home food for us all. They have no sister, so I could keep their lodge, and cook their food, and make their moccasins."

Her grandmother thought that was a fine idea, so she helped Red Leaf select seven of her nicest robes, and seven

33

pairs of her best moccasins. These she carried over to the lodge of the seven brothers.

The six brothers were hunting, and Moksois was down at the creek getting water when she came to the lodge, but she went in, anyway, and put one of the robes and a pair of moccasins on each of the seven beds. When he got back with the water, she was stirring the pot of soup on the fire. They talked, and then he saw the robes and the moccasins.

"Where did these fine moccasins and robes come from?" he asked.

"I brought them. I thought it would be a good thing for us all if I became your sister," Red Leaf answered, still stirring the soup.

"It suits me," Moksois said. "But I'll have to ask my brothers about it."

When the brothers came home from the hunt and found the fine new robes and moccasins, and learned that Red Leaf wanted to be their sister, they thought it was a good arrangement.

So that was the way it was, from then on. They all lived together, very comfortably. The brothers hunted, and Red Leaf took care of the meat they brought home, and made their robes and moccasins, and Moksois helped by bringing in water, and keeping plenty of wood for the fire.

But there came a day when everything was changed. Moksois took his bow and arrows and went out to hunt chipmunks. He wandered farther from the lodge than he thought. While he was gone, a giant buffalo bull came to the lodge and took Red Leaf and ran away with her.

He was the Double-Teethed Bull, strange mysterious bull, strongest of all the buffalo. He was different from the other buffalo, for he had teeth in his upper and in his lower jaw, and he ruled over them.

When Moksois returned to the lodge, he found it partly torn down, and the tracks of the great bull coming in and going out. He was very much afraid. Tears ran down his face while he searched for his sister. When he saw his brothers coming home from the hunt, he ran to them, crying, "A great bull has stolen our sister."

The brothers knew the tracks were those of the great Double-Teethed Bull. They began to mourn and cry. "What can we do to save our sister? The Double-Teethed Bull is so powerful we can do nothing against him. He cannot be killed."

At last, one said, "We can't just sit here. Let's get busy and build four strong corrals, one inside the other. Then we'll go and try to get our sister away from him. That way, if we can get her, we will have some strong place to bring her."

This they did, piling big logs together and bracing them like a fort. When all four were finished, little Moksois went out and gathered anthills and brought them back in his robe. He scattered the ants and sand in a line all around the inside of the smallest corral.

Then the seven brothers followed the tracks of their sister and the great bull for a long time. At last they came to the top of a high hill, from which they could look far across the plain. There they saw a great herd of buffalo, covering the plain as far as the eye could see. In the center of the herd was a large open space, and in the open space sat their sister, with the great bull lying on the ground close by. No other buffalo were near them.

The brothers had brought their medicine sacks with them. One was made from the skin of a blackbird, one from that of a crow, one from a coyote skin, and one from the skin of a tiny yellow bird. Little Moksois' medicine sack was made of tanned buffalo hide, made in the shape of a half-moon, and he carried the skin of a gopher inside it.

The eldest brother took the blackbird skin in his hand, and it changed into a live blackbird. He told the bird to fly down and try to get close enough to their sister to tell her they were there.

He flew close to Red Leaf, where she sat on the ground, half-covered by her robe. He tried to talk to her, but the

35

great bull saw him there and rumbled, "Blackbird, what are you trying to do? Are you a spy? Go away, or I will look at you and you will fall to the ground, dead." The blackbird was afraid of his power, so he flew back to the brothers.

The second brother sent the coyote that came alive from the coyote-skin medicine sack. The coyote was very clever. He slipped around far to the south, and came up on the other side of the herd. Then he went limping through the buffalo, acting as though he were sick and crippled.

But the Double-Teethed Bull was not fooled. He shook his heavy horns at him and said, "Coyote, I think you are a spy. Go away, before I look at you and you die. . . ."

So Coyote was afraid to stay. He went back to the brothers. This time they tried the crow. He flew in close, lighting on the ground and pecking as though gathering food, then flying a little closer and lighting again. But the bull suspected him. "Go away, crow. Don't come any closer. You're trying to do something bad. I think I'll just look at you. Then you will fall down dead. . . ." Crow didn't wait. He flew away, back to the brothers, waiting on the hill.

The last to go was the tiny yellow bird. He was so tiny that he crept along through the grass, among the buffalo, without any of them seeing him, even the great bull. He slipped under Red Leaf's robe and said to her, "Red Leaf, your brothers are yonder on the hill. They will try to save you. They sent me to tell you what to do. Just cover yourself all over with your robe, and pretend to go to sleep. Then wait."

The great bull snorted, and rumbled in his throat, but he didn't see the little yellow bird as he crept back through the herd. When he got back to the hill, the brothers took council among themselves. Moksois said, "Now it is my turn to do something. Everyone be quiet. I will try to put the Double-Teethed Bull to sleep so we can do something."

So he lay down on the ground with his half-moon medicine sack by his head and shut his eyes. Everyone kept very still, waiting. After a time, he opened his eyes and arose. "Blackbird, fly down and see if the bull is asleep," he said.

When the blackbird came back, he said he'd seen the great bull, sleeping soundly with his nose against the ground.

"That is good," said Moksois. "I am to blame for the Double-Teethed Bull stealing our sister. Now I will get her back. All of you wait here, but be ready to run away when I get back."

He opened his half-moon medicine sack and took the gopher skin out and laid it on the ground. Instantly, it became a live gopher, and started to dig with its long sharp claws. Moksois stayed right beside the gopher and followed it into the hole it was digging.

The gopher made a tunnel straight to where Red Leaf lay, covered by her robe. Moksois came up under her robe and took her by the hand and led her back along the gopher hole to where the brothers waited.

They took their sister, and as fast as they could, they ran toward home, to the shelter of the strong corrals they had built. But Moksois stayed behind, to keep watch on the herd. He wanted to see what happened when the great bull found Red Leaf gone. He felt very brave. "I will stay here and watch," he said. "I am not afraid. Let the Double-Teethed Bull look at me. He can't kill me with one of his looks."

The great bull heaved himself to his feet and shook himself all over. Then he walked over to Red Leaf's robe, still spread out on the ground over the gopher hole, and sniffed at it. When he saw she was gone, he bellowed and pawed the ground, throwing clouds of dust into the air. He tossed and hooked the robe with his sharp horns until he tore it to shreds.

All the buffalo were excited and milling around, pawing and bellowing. Then the bull saw the gopher hole. He sniffed at it, then began to run back over the ground the

37

same direction Moksois and Red Leaf had gone through the tunnel. All the other buffalo followed him, charging at a great speed; heads down, stirring up such a cloud of dust that it was like the smoke from a prairie fire.

Moksois watched them from the hill, but before they got too near, he put an arrow in his bow and shot it as far as he could, toward home. The instant the arrow touched the ground, Moksois was beside it. That was part of his power. He kept shooting his arrows until he reached the lodge.

"Get ready, the buffalo are coming," he cried. And they all got inside the log corrals and kept watch. In a little while, the great herd of buffalo came in sight, galloping over the plain, with the huge bull out in front. When they saw the corrals, they stopped and waited while an old cow walked slowly nearer.

"Come back with me, Red Leaf. The Double-Teethed Bull wants you," she called to them. "If you don't return, he will come and get you himself."

Moksois said, "Tell him to come, if he dares." But before she had gone very far, he shot the old cow, and she fell to the ground. Three other messengers came, asking Red Leaf to come back to the Double-Teethed Bull, and making threats. Each time Moksois gave them the same answer. Each time he shot them before they got back to the great bull. Only the last one got near enough to give him Moksois' message.

Then the great bull was terribly angry. He pranced and pawed. He hooked the ground and bellowed defiance. Head down, he charged the corral at a fast gallop, the herd thundering behind.

"Come out," he roared to the girl. "Come out. Don't you know who I am?"

Red Leaf was trembling and crying. She begged her brothers to let her go. "He will kill you all. Let me go. . . . It may save you . . ."

But Moksois said, "Don't be afraid. Don't cry. I will kill the bull."

38

When the Double-Teethed Bull heard Moksois say that, he was furious. He charged the corral and hooked his horns in the logs, tossing them aside like sticks. The churning, bellowing herd charged the other corrals, one after another, scattering the logs like straws in the wind. But when they came to the place where Moksois had made the line inside with the anthills, every grain of sand had become a big rock, making a strong rock corral, that stopped the buffalo charge.

Again and again the buffalo charged the wall, hurling the great stones in every direction, like pebbles. The eldest brother said, "Even these rocks can't stand against him. He will be inside, next time. . . ."

Their sister cried, "Let me go . . . let me go outside, or he will kill you all."

But Moksois said again, "Don't be afraid. Stay here. I still have power . . ." Then he shot his arrow straight up into the air, just as high as he could shoot it. And as high as it went, there stood a tall tree, reaching into the sky.

"Now hurry, climb up there," he cried, helping his sister into the tree. Quickly, all the brothers climbed up into the branches. But just as Moksois climbed to the lowest limb, the Double-Teethed Bull broke through the rocks with a terrible bellow that shook the hills.

He charged and charged the tree, tearing off great slivers with his sharp horns. But just as fast as he tossed a piece of wood aside, it joined back to the tree the same as it had been before.

Moksois only waited to shoot his last arrow at the powerful bull, before he followed his brothers and his sister up and up the tree, until they went into the sky. There they became the seven stars. The girl is the head star, and the little one, off to one side by itself, is little Moksois, still keeping guard.

In the Beginning

In the beginning there was nothing but soft darkness, and Raven beat and beat with his wings until the darkness packed itself down into solid earth. Then there was only the icy black ocean and a narrow strip of shoreline. But people came soon to live along the coast. And Raven felt sorry for them, poor, sickly things, who never had any sunshine. They lived by chewing on nuts and leaves, and crushed the roots of the alder trees for something to drink.

"I must help them," thought Raven; and he flew down to earth, calling, "*Ga, ga, ga!*" and gathered the people together. Like ghosts, they were, shadowy and pale in the misty darkness.

"Raven has come!" they told each other. "It is Raven-Who-Sets-Things-Right."

The poor things were encouraged, and they gathered round to see what he would do.

Raven plucked a branch from an alder, and scattered the leaves on the surface of a pool. At once the leaves were sucked under, and the water started to bubble. After the pool had boiled for a moment, the surface cleared and fish began to jump there. So that was how Raven gave the people fish.

But now that they had fish to eat, they were thirstier than

ever. They called on Raven, and down he came, and the people said, "Here is Raven-Who-Sets-Things-Right."

Raven knew that there was only one spring of fresh water in all the world. A man named Ganook had built his house around it, and refused to give any away.

"Maybe," thought Raven, "I can drink enough to carry some back to the people."

So he went to the house and asked to come in, and Ganook was very glad to have his company. Raven sat down and made polite conversation, and pretty soon he asked for a drink of water.

"Very well," said Ganook grudgingly, and showed him the spring, a crystal pool welling up in a basin of rock.

"Don't drink it all!" Ganook warned him. "You know that's the only fresh water in all the world."

Raven knew it well; that was what he had come for. But he said, "Just a sip!" and drank until he staggered.

"Hold on there, Raven!" cried Ganook. "Are you trying to drink the well dry?"

That was just what Raven was trying to do, but he passed it off lightly. He made himself comfortable close to the fire and said, "Ganook, let me tell you a story."

Then Raven started out on a long dull story about four dull brothers who went on a long dull journey. As he went along he made up dull things to add to it, and Ganook's eyelids drooped, and Raven spoke softly, and more and more slowly, and Ganook's chin dropped on his chest.

"So then," said Raven gently, with his eyes on Ganook, "on and on through the long gray valley through the soft gray fog went the four tall gray brothers. And now, snore!" And Ganook began to snore.

Quick as a thought, Raven darted to the spring and stuck his beak into the water. But no sooner had he lifted his head to swallow than Ganook started up with a terrible snort, and said, "Go on, go on, I'm listening! I'm not asleep." Then he shook his head and blinked his eyes and said, "Where are you, Raven? What are you doing?"

41

"Just walking around for exercise," Raven assured him, and back he went, and in a low, unchanging voice he went on with the dull story of the four brothers. No sooner had he started than Ganook began to nod, and his chin dropped down, and he jerked it back and opened his eyes and scowled at Raven, and nodded his head and said, "Go on! What next?" and his head dropped down upon his chest.

"So on and on," said Raven slowly, "over the hills, went the four tall gray brothers. The air was thick and gray around them. Fog was stealing softly over the mountains. Fog before them, fog behind them, soft, cloudy fog. And now, snore!" And Ganook began to snore.

Quietly Raven slipped to the spring, and, *glub*, *glub*, *glub*, he drank up the water until the pool was dry. But as he lifted his head for a last long gulp, Ganook leaped up and saw what he was doing.

"So, Raven!" shouted Ganook. "You think you can lull me to sleep and steal my water!"

He picked up his club and started to chase Raven round and round the fire. Raven would run a few steps and flap his big wings and rise a few inches off the floor. Then with a last tremendous flap he went sailing towards the open smoke hole. But he had swallowed so much water that he stuck fast in the opening, and there he struggled, while Ganook shouted, "You squint-eyed Raven, I've got you now, Raven! You miserable thief!" And Ganook threw green alder logs on the fire and made a great smoke which came billowing up and almost choked Raven to death.

Raven hung there, strangling and struggling, until at last he pulled free with a mighty wrench and went wobbling heavily across the sky. He was so heavy he flew in a crooked line, and as he flew he spurted little streams of water from his bill. These became rivers, first the Nass and the Sitka, then the Taku and the Iskut and the Stikine. Since Raven flew in a crooked line, all the rivers are crooked as snakes. Here and there he scattered single drops, and these became narrow creeks and salmon pools.

42

And so Raven brought fresh water to the people—but he bore the mark of that smoke hole ever after. He had gone to Ganook as a great, white, snowy creature, but from that day on, Raven was black, as black as the endless sky of the endless night.

Raven Lets Out the Daylight

Now Raven had made the rivers and filled them with fish but still people suffered. They had to do all their fishing in the dark, and they fished all the time, for there was nothing else to eat. Raven felt sorry for them, poking about in the everlasting darkness. So down he came, saying, "I am Raven-Who-Sets-Things-Right."

Raven knew that the Sun and the Moon and the Stars were hidden in the house of the Old-One-at-the-Source-of-the-River. He was determined to steal this light and give it to the people.

So Raven turned himself into a little baby and had himself born of the only daughter of the Old-One-at-the-Source-of-the-River. But he was no ordinary baby. On the second day he stood up in his basket; he crawled on the third day and walked on the fourth, and although he never said a word but *"Ga!"* the Old-One was even more doting and proud than grandfathers are today.

"Look at those eyes!" he said. "Sharp as a raven's!" But he never suspected that Raven himself had become a member of the family.

One thing bothered the Old-One and his daughter: the

baby refused to eat. They tried him on deer fat, mutton fat, and tallow, for inside that house was all the wealth of future generations. Coming from above as Raven did, he had no need to eat. But although the baby was growing fast, his mother was sure he was going to die unless he started to eat. So she tried a trick. She knew that anyone who ate the fish called bullhead would be hungry ever after. The baby liked to sit with them and chew a piece of fat, so she folded a shred of bullhead in the fat, and Raven swallowed it down.

All at once the baby started to cry as human babies do, stuffing his fingers into his mouth and making sucking noises.

"Can it be true?" his mother cried. "I believe my baby is hungry!"

She gave him food, and the baby ate, and a few minutes later he was hungry again. This went on all day and all week, and soon the Old-One began to fret for fear he would use up all his provisions.

Then came a new trouble. High in the rafters, the sharp eyes of Raven discovered what he had come for. Three great bags swung there in the shadows, and he figured they were just big enough to hold the Sun, the Moon, and the Stars.

"*Ga!*" said the baby, starting to cry, and he stretched his fat little arms toward the three great bags. His mother dandled him and rocked him and clucked in his ear, but nothing would make him stop.

"Father," said the Old-One's daughter at last, "why can't the baby play with the smallest bag?"

"No!" said the Old-One, but the baby kept on crying, and at last he could stand it no longer and gave him the bag.

The baby was quiet, rolling the bag about on the floor behind his mother. Then all at once he pulled the draw-string, and *whoosh!* the Stars swept up through the smoke hole and scattered to their places in the sky.

For some time after that the grandfather was angry, and the poor mother kept Raven as quiet as she could with enormous quantities of food. The shred of bullhead had done its work; Raven was a ravenous eater from that day forward.

Between feedings he did nothing but cry and stretch out his arms toward the remaining two bags that swung against the rafters. He cried until his eyes turned around in his head, and his mother was frantic with worry.

"You're not going to have them!" the Old-One thundered, but at last he took the second bag down from the hook and gave it to his grandson.

Raven was quiet, rolling the bag about on the earthen floor behind them. Then secretly he loosened the string, and *whisk!* the silver disk of the Moon went spinning through the smoke hole.

The Old-One was sad, because now he had lost all but the last of his sacred treasures. And still the baby cried and cried as he stretched out his arms for the Sun bag. His mother was distracted, and the Old-One was afraid the baby was going to die.

"Take it, then!" he shouted, and threw him the bag—but first he tightened the cord.

Raven worked and worked on the knot, but there was nothing he could do. So, "*Ga, ga, ga!*" he changed back to a Raven, seized the bag, and escaped through the smoke hole.

He flew and he flew until he came to the crooked river where all the people were fishing. And this time when Raven looked at the piles of fish gleaming like silver in the darkness, he was ravenously hungry.

"Give me some of your fish," he said to the people. "I'm feeling very hungry."

As soon as Raven wanted something for himself, the ungrateful people refused him.

"Catch your own fish," they told him rudely. "We have scarcely enough for ourselves."

46

"Come, now, just a little, and I'll let out the daylight!"

"Let out the daylight? You? You're Raven; you haven't any daylight. Get away!"

Raven went on down the river a bit, and begged fish of the next little group, for by now he was starving. But the answer was the same, on and on down the river, until he came to the last village, near the coast.

"Ga, ga, ga!" croaked Raven weakly. "Give me some fish, and I will let out the daylight!"

"Come, now, Raven; you can't let out the daylight! But all the same we'll help you if you're hungry." And they threw him a small pile of fish, which he devoured in a twinkling.

Then Raven said, "Cover your eyes with your fingers, now, for I'm letting out the daylight!"

They covered their eyes, and Raven tore at the Sun bag with his beak. First he made a small tear in the bag, and the rays of the Sun shot out like jagged lightning. Then he caught the great round disk in his beak, and ripped it out of the bag!

A wave of light rushed over the world, and in all the canoes, up and down the river, the fishermen jumped to their feet. Canoes capsized on every side as they tried to shield their eyes. Some of the people dived overboard, and some of them leaped for the shore. Those that took to the water became seals and otters and sea lions, and those that took to the forest became forest creatures. And only those that gave Raven the fish continued to be men.

But instead of the weak, sickly creatures that had lived before in the world of darkness, these men were strong and vigorous and daring. They launched their canoes on the open ocean, and pitted their strength against the strength of sharks and whales. The drooping trees stretched up tall in the forest, and pale leaves curled like the fronds of ferns, opened to drink the sunlight. Flowers sprang up in the grass like stars, and glittering insects hummed and drummed all day in the golden sunshine.

Then back flew Raven to the Source of the River to see what the Old-One thought about it now. He perched on a tree near the house of the Old-One and called to the Old-One's daughter.

"Come out, come out, my mother," said Raven, "and see what I've done to the world."

She came out, frightened.

"I've seen what you've done, and I think it is right, but my father is still in a rage. He sits in the house in his conjuror's hat and tries to conjure you back; and now he's done it. So fly away, Raven, before it's too late, or the Old-One will have his revenge upon us all."

"I won't fly away until he comes outdoors to see what the world is like."

His mother implored him to fly away home, but boldly he entered the house of the Old-One, with his mother following after. At first it was dark. He could make out nothing but the feeble flicker of the embers. But there on the bench, with his chin on his fists, glowering, sat the Old-One.

"Who is it that comes?" he growled without turning, and Raven answered, "Your grandson."

The Old-One sprang to his feet with a roar of anger.

"Grandson, you say! You're no grandson of mine, you Raven! You stole the Sun!"

"Come to the door, Old-One, and I'll show you what the Sun has done for the world!"

"Done for it, has it?" the Old-One shouted. "I'll show you what I can do!"

The Old-One gave his conjuror's hat a twist, and water gushed out of the top like a whirlpool and splashed in a circle on the floor and made a pool.

"Father, father!" cried Raven's mother. "Stop the water quickly, I beg you!"

But he gave his hat another twist, and the water gushed faster than ever. It filled the center of the huge house, and Raven and his mother climbed to the level of the rooms along the back. And as the house was filling the world was flooded, to the level of the foothills. The people and the forest creatures fled to the hills to escape the rising waters.

Then Raven's mother cried, "Father, I beg you! Stop it! Stop the flood!"

But the Old-One twisted his hat again, and the water gushed out in a torrent. Raven and his mother climbed up to a narrow shelf close under the roof. At the same time the whole earth was flooded, and the people and animals were crowded together on the tops of the highest mountains.

"Father!" cried Raven's mother again. "Let the waters go down!"

But the Old-One sat there and twisted his hat, and the waters filled the house to the very rafters. Then Raven changed his mother to a silver fish, and they both escaped through the smoke hole.

Raven flew out over a desolate waste, lashed by the slanting rain. All of the lush and sunshiny world had been washed away by the flood. The whole round circle was a tossing ocean, under a lowering sky. On flew Raven, heading for the mountains, and he saw that the top of the highest mountain was now an island in the waste. The dark figures of wolves and bears were slinking among the rocks; and as Raven flew over he heard a faint crying, a lonely sound almost lost in the roar of the tempest.

He circled back and found four small children, cowering for fear of the hungry beasts that were trapped on the mountain with them. Only these four little children were left, of all the flourishing tribes that had peopled the earth.

So Raven scooped them up with his claws, and flew up and up, to thrust his strong beak into the solid floor of the sky. He hung there until the rain stopped, and sheltered the four little children under his wings.

When a watery sun drank up the clouds, he called on his friend the Frog to come and dropped the children down on her broad green back. There they floated for twenty days more, until the water ran off the mountains in torrents and the children could wade ashore.

So it was that Raven saved the children from the flood, and these four children lived to be the parents of future generations.

How Coyote Stole Fire

Long ago, when man was newly come into the world, there were days when he was the happiest creature of all. Those were the days when spring brushed across the willow tails, or when his children ripened with the blueberries in the sun of summer, or when the goldenrod bloomed in the autumn haze.

But always the mists of autumn evenings grew more chill, and the sun's strokes grew shorter. Then man saw winter moving near, and he became fearful and unhappy. He was afraid for his children, and for the grandfathers and grandmothers who carried in their heads the sacred tales of the tribe. Many of these, young and old, would die in the long, ice-bitter months of winter.

Coyote, like the rest of the People, had no need for fire. So he seldom concerned himself with it, until one spring day when he was passing a human village. There the women were singing a song of mourning for the babies and the old ones who had died in the winter. Their voices moaned like the west wind through a buffalo skull, prickling the hairs on Coyote's neck.

"Feel how the sun is now warm on our backs," one of the men was saying. "Feel how it warms the earth and makes these stones hot to the touch. If only we could have had a small piece of the sun in our teepees during the winter."

Coyote, overhearing this, felt sorry for the men and women. He also felt that there was something he could do to help them. He knew of a faraway mountain-top where the three Fire Beings lived. These Beings kept fire to themselves, guarding it carefully for fear that man might somehow acquire it and become as strong as they. Coyote saw that he could do a good turn for man at the expense of these selfish Fire Beings.

So Coyote went to the mountain of the Fire Beings and crept to its top, to watch the way that the Beings guarded their fire. As he came near, the Beings leaped to their feet and gazed searchingly round their camp. Their eyes glinted like bloodstones, and their hands were clawed like the talons of the great black vulture.

"What's that? What's that I hear?" hissed one of the Beings.

"A thief, skulking in the bushes!" screeched another.

The third looked more closely, and saw Coyote. But he had gone to the mountain-top on all-fours, so the Being thought she saw only an ordinary coyote slinking among the trees.

"It is no one, it is nothing!" she cried, and the other two looked where she pointed and also saw only a grey coyote. They sat down again by their fire and paid Coyote no more attention.

So he watched all day and night as the Fire Beings guarded their fire. He saw how they fed it pine cones and dry branches from the sycamore trees. He saw how they stamped furiously on runaway rivulets of flame that sometimes nibbled outwards on edges of dry grass. He saw also how, at night, the Beings took turns to sit by the fire. Two would sleep while one was on guard; and at certain times the Being by the fire would get up and go into their teepee, and another would come out to sit by the fire.

Coyote saw that the Beings were always jealously watchful of their fire except during one part of the day. That was in the earliest morning, when the first winds of dawn arose on the mountains. Then the Being by the fire would hurry, shivering, into the teepee calling, "Sister, sister, go out and watch the fire." But the next Being would always be slow to go out for her turn, her head spinning with sleep and the thin dreams of dawn.

Coyote, seeing all this, went down the mountain and spoke to some of his friends among the People. He told them of hairless man, fearing the cold and death of winter. And he told them of the Fire Beings, and the warmth and brightness of the flame. They all agreed that man should have fire, and they all promised to help Coyote's undertaking.

Then Coyote sped again to the mountain-top. Again the Fire Beings leaped up when he came close, and one cried out, "What's that? A thief, a thief!"

But again the others looked closely, and saw only a grey coyote hunting among the bushes. So they sat down again and paid him no more attention.

Coyote waited through the day, and watched as night fell and two of the Beings went off to the teepee to sleep. He watched as they changed over at certain times all the night long, until at last the dawn winds rose.

Then the Being on guard called, "Sister, sister, get up and watch the fire."

And the Being whose turn it was climbed slow and sleepy from her bed, saying, "Yes, yes, I am coming. Do not shout so."

But before she could come out of the teepee, Coyote lunged from the bushes, snatched up a glowing portion of fire, and sprang away down the mountainside.

Screaming, the Fire Beings flew after him. Swift as Coyote ran, they caught up with him, and one of them

54

reached out a clutching hand. Her fingers touched only the tip of the tail, but the touch was enough to turn the hairs white, and coyote tail-tips are white still. Coyote shouted, and flung the fire away from him. But the others of the People had gathered at the mountain's foot, in case they were needed. Squirrel saw the fire falling, and caught it, putting it on her back and fleeing away through the tree-tops. The fire scorched her back so painfully that her tail curled up and back, as squirrels' tails still do today.

The Fire Beings then pursued Squirrel, who threw the fire to Chipmunk. Chattering with fear, Chipmunk stood still as if rooted until the Beings were almost upon her. Then, as she turned to run, one Being clawed at her, tearing down the length of her back and leaving three stripes that are to be seen on chipmunks' backs even today. Chipmunk threw the fire to Frog, and the Beings turned towards him. One of the Beings grasped his tail, but Frog gave a mighty leap and tore himself free, leaving his tail behind in the Being's hand—which is why frogs have had no tails ever since.

As the Beings came after him again, Frog flung the fire on to Wood. And Wood swallowed it.

The Fire Beings gathered round, but they did not know how to get the fire out of Wood. They promised it gifts, sang to it and shouted at it. They twisted it and struck it and tore it with their knives. But Wood did not give up the fire. In the end, defeated, the Beings went back to their mountain-top and left the People alone.

But Coyote knew how to get fire out of Wood. And he went to the village of men and showed them how. He showed them the trick of rubbing two dry sticks together, and the trick of spinning a sharpened stick in a hole made in another piece of wood. So man was from then on warm and safe through the killing cold of winter.

How Glooskap Found the Summer

Long ago a mighty race of Indians lived near the sunrise, and they called themselves Wawaniki—Children of Light. Glooskap was their master. He was kind to his people and did many great deeds for them.

Once in Glooskap's day it grew extremely cold. Snow and ice covered everything. Fires would not give enough warmth. The corn would not grow. His people were perishing from cold and famine.

Glooskap set forth for the far north where all was ice. Here in a wigwam he found the great giant Winter. It was Winter's icy breath that had frozen the land.

Glooskap entered the wigwam and sat down. Winter gave him a pipe, and as they smoked the giant told tales of olden times when he reigned everywhere and all the land was silent, white, and beautiful. His frost charm fell upon Glooskap and as the giant talked on, Glooskap fell asleep. For six months he slept like a bear, then the charm left him. He was too strong for it and awoke.

Soon now Glooskap's talebearer, the Loon, a wild bird who lived on the lakeshores, brought him strange news. He described a country far to the south where it was always warm. There lived the all-powerful Summer who could easily overcome the giant Winter. To save his people from cold and famine and death, Glooskap decided to find her.

Far off to the southern seashores he went. He sang the magic song which whales obey and up came an old friend—a whale who served as his carrier when he wished to go out to sea.

This whale had a law for travelers. She always said: "You must shut your eyes while I carry you. If you do not, I am sure to go aground on a reef or sand-bar and be unable to get off. You could be drowned."

Glooskap got on the whale's back and for many days they traveled together. Each day the water grew warmer and the air softer and sweeter, for it came from spicy shores. The odors were no longer those of salt, but of fruits and flowers.

Soon they found themselves in shallow water. Down in the sand clams were singing a song of warning: "Keep out to sea, for the water here is shallow."

The whale asked Glooskap, who understood the language of all creatures: "What do they say?"

Glooskap, wishing to land at once, only replied: "They tell you to hurry, for a storm is coming."

The whale hurried on accordingly until she was close to land. Now Glooskap did the forbidden; he opened his left eye, to peep. At once the whale stuck hard on to the beach so that Glooskap, leaping from her head, was able to walk ashore on dry land.

Thinking she could never get away, the whale became angry. But Glooskap put one end of his strong bow against the whale's jaw and, taking the other end in his hands, placed his feet against the high bank. With a mighty push, he sent her out into the deep water.

Far inland strode Glooskap and found it warmer at every step. In the forest he came upon a beautiful woman, dancing in the center of a group of young girls. Her long brown

58

hair was crowned with flowers and her arms filled with blossoms. She was Summer.

Glooskap knew that here at last was the one who by her charms could melt old Winter's heart. He leaped to catch her and would not let her go. Together they journeyed the long way back to the lodge of old Winter.

Winter welcomed Glooskap but he planned to freeze him to sleep again. This time, however, Glooskap did the talking. His charm proved the stronger one and soon sweat began to run down Winter's face. He knew that his power was gone and the charm of Frost broken. His icy tent melted away.

Summer now used her own special power and everything awoke. The grass grew green and the snow ran down the rivers, carrying away the dead leaves. Old Winter wept to see his power taken away.

But Summer said, "Now that I have proved I am more powerful than you, I give you all the country to the far north for your own, and there I shall never disturb you. Six months of every year you may return to Glooskap's country and reign as before, but you are to be less severe with your power. During the other six months, I will come back from the South and rule the land."

Old Winter could do nothing but accept this. So it is that he appears in Glooskap's country each year to reign for six months, but with a softer rule. When he comes, Summer runs home to her warm south land. When at the end of six months she returns to drive old Winter away, she awakens the north and gives it the joys that only she can bestow.

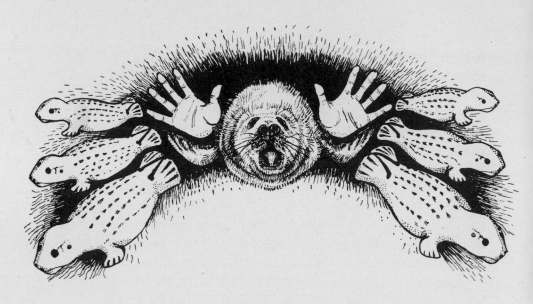

Sedna, the Sea Goddess

The Petrels, proud birds that they are, live on the highest parts of the cliffs. From their peaks they swirl out like snowflakes, looking down on the rolling noisiness of Razor Bills who build their nests halfway up, and the Gulls and the little Kittiwakes who are content to nest at the bottom.

Once, long, long ago, there was a Petrel who was so proud that he could find no mate that pleased him among his own kind, so he decided that he would marry a human being.

With a little magic, the Petrel gave himself a human form. Then, wanting to look his best, he got some fine seal skins and made a beautiful parka. Now he looked very handsome, but his eyes were still the eyes of a bird, so he made some spectacles from thin pieces of walrus tusk. These spectacles had only narrow slits to look through, and hid the Petrel's eyes completely.

In this disguise, he went out in his kayak to find a wife.

In a skin-covered tent beside the sea there lived a beauti-

ful girl named Sedna, who had many brothers but no
sisters, and her father was a widower. Many men had
come to her to ask her to marry them—men from her own
tribe and other tribes—but Sedna refused to marry. She
was as proud in her way as the Petrel, and could find no
man who pleased her.

Then the Petrel came, appearing as a handsome stranger
in a beautiful sealskin parka. Instead of bringing his kayak
up onto the beach, he stayed in it at the edge of the surf and
called out to Sedna to come to him. This interested Sedna,
as no other suitor had done such a thing, but she would not
go to him.

Then he began to sing to her:

> "Come to me,
> Come into the land of the birds
> Where there is never hunger,
> Where my tent is made of beautiful skins
> You will have a necklace of ivory
> And sleep in the skins of bears.
> Your lamps will be always filled with oil
> And your pot with meat."

The song was so beautiful that Sedna could not refuse.
She packed her belongings in a sealskin bag; she stepped
out of the tent and she walked down across the beach and
got into the stranger's kayak. They sailed out over the sea,
away from Sedna's home and her father and brothers.

The Petrel made a home for Sedna on the rocky cliff.
Every day he caught fish for her, telling her that they were
young seals, and for a while Sedna was happy, because the
Petrel had enchanted her. But one day the Petrel's spectacles fell off and for the first time Sedna looked into her
husband's eyes. In that moment the spell was broken. She
realized all at once that she was married to a bird, and she
saw that her home was a nest on a barren cliff. For the first
time she felt the sting of the sea spray and the lashing
winds.

Sedna wept with grief and despair, and the Petrel, although he loved her, could not console her.

In the meantime, Sedna's father and brothers had grown more and more lonely, with no woman to cook their meat and sew their clothing and keep the oil burning in their lamps. They set out in their boat in the direction that the stranger had taken Sedna.

When they came to the cliff where Sedna lived, the Petrel was away hunting, and Sedna was alone. When she saw her family, she went running down to them, weeping, and in a rush told them all that had happened to her. Her brothers immediately lifted her into the boat and they began paddling as rapidly as possible back toward their own coast.

They had not been gone long when the Petrel returned to the nest. He looked everywhere for Sedna, and he called for her, his cry a long and lonely sound that was lost in the wind and the sound of the sea. Other Petrels answered him; they told him where Sedna had gone. Spreading his wings, he soared out over the sea and was soon flying over the boat that was carrying Sedna back to her home. This made the brothers nervous, and they paddled faster. As they skimmed over the water, the Petrel became angry. He began to beat his wings against the wind, making it whirl and shriek, and making the waves leap higher and higher. In minutes the sea was black with storm, and the waves so wild that the boat was in danger of turning over. Then Sedna's brothers and father realized that the Petrel was such a powerful spirit that even the sea was angry because his bride was being taken from him. They decided that they must sacrifice Sedna to the sea in order to save their own lives. They picked her up and threw her into the icy water.

Sedna, blue with cold, came up to the surface and grabbed at the side of the boat with fingers that were turning to ice. Her brothers, out of their minds with fear, hit at her hands with a paddle, and her fingertips broke off like icicles and fell back into the sea, where they turned into

seals and swam away. Coming up again, Sedna tried once more to catch hold of the boat, and again her brothers hit at her hands with the paddle. The second joints of her fingers, breaking off and falling into the water, turned into *ojuk*, ground seals. Two more times Sedna attempted to take hold of the side of the boat, and each time her terrified brothers hit her hands, and the third joints of her fingers turned into walrus and the thumbs became whales. Then Sedna sank to the bottom of the sea. The storm died down, and the brothers finally brought their boat to land, but a great wave followed them and drowned all of them.

Sedna became a powerful spirit, in control of the sea creatures who sprang from her fingers. Sometimes she sends storms and wrecks kayaks. The people fear her, and hold ceremonies in her honor, and on especially serious occasions—as when she causes famines by keeping the seals from being caught by the hunters—the *angakok*, or conjurer, goes on a spirit journey to Sedna's home at the bottom of the sea, to arrange her hair.

Sedna wears her hair in two braids, each as thick as an arm, but since she has no fingers, she cannot plait her own hair, and this is the service she appreciates most of all. So when the *angakok* comes to her and arranges her hair for her, she is so grateful that she sends some of the seals and other animals to the hunters so that they may have food.

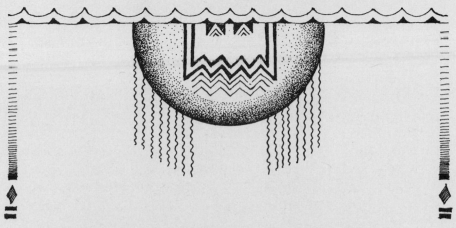

How Saynday Got the Sun

Saynday was a culture hero of the Kiowa Indians, one who "made the world the way it was".

Saynday was coming along, and all the world was black. There was no sun on this side of the world, and the people were in darkness. The sun belonged to the people on the other side, and they kept it close by, so that no one could get it away from them.

As Saynday was coming along, he met some of the animals. There were Fox and Deer and Magpie. They were all sitting together by a prairie dog hole, talking things over.

"What's the matter?" said Saynday.

"We don't like this world," said Fox.

"What's wrong with this world?" said Saynday.

"We don't like the darkness," said Deer.

"What's wrong with the darkness?" said Saynday.

"It won't let things live and be happy," said Magpie.

"I guess we'd better do something about it," said Saynday.

So the four of them sat by the prairie dog hole, and they thought and they thought and they thought and they thought. They were so quiet that the prairie dog stuck his

65

head out of the ground, and when he saw them sitting there, he stayed still and joined in the thinking.

"There is a sun," said Saynday at last.

"Where is it?" said Fox.

"It's on the other side of the world," said Saynday.

"What's it doing there?" said Deer.

"The people who have it won't let it go," said Saynday.

"What good is it to us, then?" said Magpie.

"Not any," said Saynday. "I guess we'd better do something about it," said Saynday.

So they sat and they sat and they thought and they thought. They none of them moved at all.

Then Saynday said, "We could go and borrow that sun."

"It wouldn't really be stealing," said Fox.

"We don't want to keep it for always," said Saynday.

"We'd give it back to them sometimes," said Deer.

"Then things could live and grow on their side of the world," said Magpie.

"But they'd live and grow on this side, too," said Saynday.

Then Saynday got busy, because he'd finished his thinking. He could begin to do things now.

"How far can you run?" he said to Fox.

"A long long way," said Fox.

"How far can you run?" he said to Deer.

"A short long way," said Deer.

"How far can you run?" he said to Magpie.

"A long short way," said Magpie.

"I can't run very far myself," said Saynday, "so I guess I'll have to take it last."

Then he lined them all out and told them what to do. Fox was to go to the village on the other side of the earth and to make friends with the people who lived there. That was the first thing to do, and that was the hardest. So Fox got ready and started out.

Fox traveled a long way, feeling his way along in the darkness. Then there was a little rim of light on the rim of the world ahead of him, like the sun coming up in the wintertime. He traveled toward the rim of light, and it got stronger and stronger till it was a whole blaze of light and filled all the sky ahead of him. Then he was up on a hill, and down below him was the village of the people who had the sun. Fox sat down on the hilltop and watched them while he made up his mind what to do.

The people were playing a game with the sun. They were lined up on two sides, and each side had four spears. They would roll the sun along the ground like a ball, and take turns throwing the spears at it. The side that hit it the most times won. One side was way ahead, and the other side was losing badly.

Fox went down the hill into the village and lay on the ground with his nose on his paws, and watched. They rolled the sun again, and the side that was ahead won two more points, and the side that was behind lost again.

So Fox said quietly, so just the captain of the losing side could hear him, "Good luck to the losers."

Nobody paid any attention, except the captain, and he just turned his head for a minute. Then they rolled the sun again, and this time the losing side won.

The captain came over and said to Fox. "Thank you for wishing us well."

"Good luck to your winning," said Fox, and this time that side won again.

Then they had some excitement. The side that had been winning before wanted to send Fox away, but the side that had been losing wanted to keep him. They argued and argued, but Fox's side was the strongest, and in the end he stayed.

Fox stayed and stayed and stayed and stayed in that village. He stayed till he knew it as well as he did his own home. He stayed till he knew the names of all the people, and what they did and where they all lived. He stayed till he knew where they kept the sun all the time, and who were the men who watched it. He stayed till he knew all the

67

rules of the game they played with the sun, and even till they let him play himself. All the time he was staying and playing, he was making his plan.

One day they had a big game. It was to decide the champions for that year. Fox was playing on the side that he had wished luck to in the beginning. Everybody else rolled the sun first because they had all been playing first, before he came. Then it was Fox's turn to roll. He took the sun in his paws the way they had taught him, and bent over as if he were going to send it along the ground. But instead of rolling it, he got a good start on his running, and he carried the sun along with him.

For just the first minute the people were so surprised to see their sun going away that they didn't know what to do. Then they were mad, and they started to run after Fox. But Fox was a fast runner and he could run a long way. That was why Saynday put him first. He ran and he ran, and at last he caught up with Deer.

Deer didn't even take time to look at the sun. He grabbed it away from Fox and started running with it himself. He ran and he ran, and just when he started to give out, he caught up with Magpie.

The sun village people were so far behind they couldn't be seen now, but Magpie didn't take any chances. He started right out with that sun, going as fast and as far away from there as he could. Just when his breath was gone, he came up to Saynday and handed the sun to him.

The sun village people were so far behind now that Saynday didn't bother to run. He just walked along with the sun over his shoulder like a big sack of meat. He walked along so easy that the others caught up with him. When they were back by their prairie dog hole, they all sat down to rest.

"Well, now we have the sun," said Saynday.

"Now we can have light," said Fox.

"Now we can see what we are doing and where we are going," said Saynday.

"Now we can travel around," said Deer.

"Now plants will come up out of the ground and grow," said Saynday.

"Now there will be trees to live in," said Magpie.

"I guess we brought light to our world," said Saynday.

But the trouble was, there was too much light. It had been dark all the time and now it was light all the time. People could travel around all right, but they got tired out because it was light and they were traveling all the time. The plants and trees could grow, but they never stopped growing. Magpie and his wife went to bed in a tree ten foot off the ground and waked up twenty feet up in the air. It was all very bothersome.

Finally the three friends went back to see Saynday.

Saynday was sitting on the ground in front of his teepee, admiring the sun shining on the ground in front of him.

"What's the matter?" he said.

"There's too much light," said Fox.

"We don't want so much," said Deer.

"We don't need so much," said Magpie.

"What can we do?" said Saynday.

"Try putting the sun somewhere else," said Fox.

"That's a good idea," said Saynday.

He put the sun in the teepee, but it kept shining right through the walls.

"Put it up off the ground," said Deer.

"All right," said Saynday, and he balanced it on top of the teepee.

Whoosh! It burned the teepee right down.

"Throw it away," said Magpie.

"All right," said Saynday. "I don't want the old thing."

And he threw it straight up into the sky, and there it stayed.

"That's a good place for it," said Fox.

"It's far enough away not to burn things," said Saynday.

"It has plenty of room to move around," said Deer.

69

"It can travel from one side of the sky to the other," said Saynday.

"Now things can grow a little at a time," said Magpie.

"Now all the people on both sides of the world can divide the light evenly," said Saynday.

And that's the way it was, and that's the way it is, to this good day.

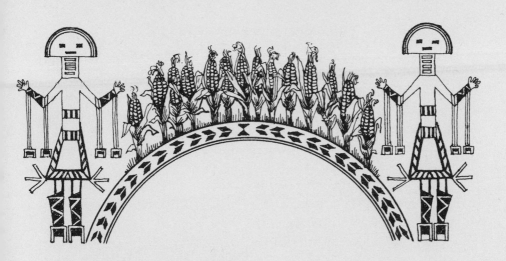

Big Long Man's Corn Patch

As soon as Big Long Man got back from the mountains he went to his garden to admire his corn and melons. He had planted a big crop for the coming winter. When he saw that half of the corn stalks had been shucked and the ears stolen, and that the biggest melons were gone off of the melon vines, he was very angry.

"Who stole my corn and melons?" he muttered to himself. "I'll catch the thief, whoever he is."

He began to scheme. The next day he built a fence around the garden. But the fence did no good. Each morning Big Long Man found more corn stalks stripped.

At last he thought up a scheme to catch the thief. He gathered a great ball of pine pitch and molded it into the shape of a man. He set the figure up in the corn field and then went to his hogan.*

That night Skunk came along to get a bit of corn for his dinner. He had heard from Badger that Big Long Man was away in the mountains. He squeezed his body under the

* A Navajo earth-covered lodge.

fence and waddled up to a clump of corn. He was just about to shuck a fat ear when he noticed a man standing by the fence. Skunk let go of the ear of corn in fright. He could see in the moonlight that the man was not Big Long Man. He waddled over to the fence and spoke to the figure.

"Who are you, in Big Long Man's corn patch?" asked Skunk.

The figure did not answer.

"Who are you?" said Skunk again, moving closer.

The figure did not answer.

"Speak!" said Skunk boldly, "or I will punch your face."

The figure did not say a word. It did not move an inch.

"Tell me who you are," said Skunk a fourth time, raising his fist, "or I will punch your face."

The figure said not a word. It was very quiet in the moonlit corn field. Even the wind had gone away.

Plup went Skunk's fist into the pine gum face. It sunk into the soft pitch, which is as sticky as glue, and there it stuck. Skunk pulled and pulled.

"If you don't let go my hand," he shouted, "I will hit you harder with my left hand."

But the pine pitch held tight.

Plup went Skunk's left hand. Now both hands stuck fast.

"Let go my hands, or I will kick you," cried Skunk, who was by this time getting mad.

The pine gum man did not let go.

Plup, Skunk gave a mighty kick with his right foot. The foot stuck too, just like the hands.

"I will kick you harder," said Skunk and *Plup* he kicked with all of his strength with his left foot. Pine gum man held that foot too. Skunk struggled but he could not get loose. Now he was in a fine plight. Every limb was held tight. He had only one more weapon, his teeth.

"I will bite your throat," he shouted and he dug his teeth into the pine gum throat.

"Ugh!" he gurgled for he could no longer say a word. His tongue and teeth were held fast in the pine pitch.

The next morning Big Long Man came to his corn patch and there was Skunk stuck onto the pine gum man. Only his tail was free, waving behind him.

"Ah!" said Big Long Man. "So it's you, Skunk, who has been stealing my corn."

"Ugh," replied Skunk. His mouth full of pine pitch.

Big Long Man pulled him away from the gum figure, tied a rope around his neck and led him to his hogan. He put a great pot of water on the stove to boil, then he took the rope off of Skunk's neck.

"Now, Skunk," he said, "go fetch wood."

Skunk went out into the back yard. Just then Fox happened to pass by. He was on his way to Big Long Man's corn patch. Skunk began to cry loudly. Fox stopped running, and pricked up his sharp ears.

"Who is crying?" he said.

"I am crying," said Skunk.

"Why?" said Fox.

"Because I have to carry wood for Big Long Man. He gives me all of the corn I want to eat, but I do not want to carry wood."

Fox was hungry. He knew that if he stole corn he was liable to get caught. "What an easy way to get corn," he thought. "I would not mind carrying wood."

Out loud he said, "Cousin, let us change places. You go home and I will carry wood for Big Long Man. I like the job. Besides, I was just on my way to steal an ear of corn down at the field."

"All right," said Skunk. "But don't eat too much corn. I have a stomach ache." He felt his fat stomach and groaned. Then he waddled happily away. Fox gathered up an armful of piñón* wood. He hurried into Big Long Man's hogan. Big Long Man looked at him in surprise.

"Well, well, Skunk, you changed into a fox, did you? That's funny."

*A low-growing pine tree bearing edible nuts.

Fox did not say a word. He was afraid he might say the wrong thing and not get any corn to eat. Big Long Man took the rope which had been around Skunk's neck and tied it around Fox's neck.

Fox sat down and waited patiently. Soon the water in the big pot began to bubble and steam. At last Fox said, "Isn't the corn cooked yet, Big Long Man?"

"Corn?" asked Big Long Man. "What corn?"

"Why the corn you are cooking for me," said Fox. "Skunk said you would feed me all of the corn I could eat if I carried wood for you."

"The rascal," said Big Long Man. "He tricked you and he tricked me. Well, Fox, you will have to pay for this." So saying he picked up Fox by the ears and set him down in the boiling water. It was so hot that it took off every hair on his body. Big Long Man left him in the pot for a minute and then he pulled him out by the ears and set him free out of doors.

"Don't be thinking you will ever get any of my corn by tricks," said Big Long Man.

Fox ran yelping toward his den. He was sore all over. Half way home he passed Red Monument. Red Monument is a tall slab of red sand stone that stands alone in a valley. On top of the rock sat Raven eating corn that he had stolen from the corn patch. At the bottom was Coyote holding on to the rock with his paws. He was watching for Raven to drop a few kernels. He glanced behind him when Fox appeared. He did not let go of the rock, however, because he thought Fox might get his place. He was surprised at Fox's appearance.

"Where is your fur, Fox?" he asked over his shoulder.

"I ate too much corn," said Fox sadly. "Don't ever eat too much corn, Coyote. It is very painful." Fox held his stomach and groaned. "Corn is very bad for one's fur. It ruined mine."

"But where did you get so much corn, cousin?" asked Coyote, still holding on to the rock.

"Didn't you hear?" asked Fox. "Why, Big Long Man is giving corn to all the animals who carry wood for him. He will give you all you can eat and more too. Just gather an armful fo piñon sticks and walk right into his hogan."

Coyote thought a moment. He was greedy. He decided to go to Big Long Man's hogan but he did not want Fox to go with him. He wanted everything for himself.

"Cousin," he said, "will you do me a favor? Will you hold this rock while I go and get a bite of corn from Big Long Man? I am very hungry and I do not dare leave this rock. It will fall and kill somebody."

"All right," said Fox, smiling to himself. "I will hold the rock. But do not eat too much." He placed his paws on the back side of the rock and Coyote let go. The next minute Coyote was running away as fast as he could toward Big Long Man's hogan. Fox laughed to himself, but after a bit he became tired of holding the rock. He decided to let it fall.

"Look out, Cousin Raven," he shouted. "The rock is going to fall." Fox let go, and jumped far away. Then he ran and did not look behind. He was afraid the rock would hit his tail. If Fox had looked behind him he would have seen the rock standing as steady as a mountain.

Presently, along came Coyote, back from Big Long Man's hogan. He was running at top speed and yowling fearfully. There was not a hair left on his body. When he came to Red Monument he saw Raven still sitting on his high perch nibbling kernels of corn.

"Where has Fox gone?" howled Coyote who was in a rage.

Raven looked down at Coyote. "Fox?" he said. "Why, Fox went home, I suppose. What did you do with your hair, Coyote?"

Coyote didn't answer. He just sat down by the foot of the rock and with his snout up in the air waited for Raven to drop a few kernels of corn.

"I'll get Fox some other day," he muttered to himself.

Poor Turkey Girl

Long ago in Mátsaki, or the Salt City, in the south-west of North America, ancestors of the Zuñi Indians kept turkeys as domestic birds. It was the custom of wealthy families who possessed large flocks to have their slaves or poor town dwellers herd them in the plains around Thunder Mountain and the mesas beyond.

At this time there lived alone near the border of the town in a tumble-down house a girl so poor that she had to become one of those who herded turkeys for a living. Poverty made her shameful to look upon, but she had a winning face and bright eyes. She had only the barest amount of food and now and then a piece of worn-out clothing. Thus she came to be called Poor Turkey Girl.

She was a humble person and longed for the kindness which she never received, but she was kind to the turkeys that she drove each day from their owners' cages to the plains. In return the turkeys obediently came at once to her every call.

One day Poor Turkey Girl, driving her turkeys down onto the plains, passed by Old Zuñi—the Middle Ant Hill of the World, so the ancients taught—and here she heard a priest proclaiming from a housetop that the Dance of the

76

Sacred Bird would take place in four days. It was an important festival at which youths and maidens delighted in dancing together.

Poor Turkey Girl had never been permitted to join or even watch these festivities. Now, again, she put aside her longing and only lamented: "Ugly and ill-clad as I am, it is impossible that I should watch or join in the Dance of the Sacred Bird." She went on driving her turkeys, and at night returned them to their owners around the town.

Every day until the time of the dance Poor Turkey Girl saw the townspeople talking and laughing as they prepared their garments and cooked delicacies for the festival. As she did her work, she chattered about this to her turkeys, not suspecting that they could understand.

But they did understand, even more than she said to them. On the fourth day, after the people of Mátsaki had departed toward Zuñi and Poor Turkey Girl was wandering around the plains as usual with her turkeys, one of the big gobblers strutted up to her. Making a fan of his tail and skirts of his wings, he puffed with importance and stretched out his neck, saying: "Maiden mother, we know your thoughts and truly we pity you. We wish that like the other people of Mátsaki you might enjoy this holiday in the town below. At night, after you have brought us safely to our cages, we have said to ourselves: "Truly, our maiden mother is as worthy to enjoy these things as any one in Mátsaki, or even in Zuñi."

"Now listen well, for I speak the speech of all the elders. When the dance has become gay and the people happy, we shall help you make yourself so beautiful that not a man, woman, or child at the dance will recognize you. The young men will wonder whence you came and long to lay hold of your hand in the circle that forms around the altar for the dance. Maiden mother, would you like to see this dance and join in it, and be merry with the best of your people?"

Poor Turkey Girl was at first surprised, but then she

77

found it natural to have the turkeys talking to her. She looked at them and said: "My beloved turkeys, how glad I am that we may speak together! But why should you tell me of things that you know I long for yet cannot possibly have?"

"Trust us," said the old gobbler, "for I speak the speech of my people. When we begin to gobble and gobble, and turn toward our home in Mátsaki, you must follow us and we shall show you what we can do for you. Only let me tell you one thing: no one knows how much happiness and good fortune may come to you if you but enjoy these pleasures moderately. But if in an excess of enjoyment, you should forget us who are your friends and depend on you, then we shall think: "Behold, our maiden mother, though so humble and poor, deserves her hard life, because were she more prosperous she would be unto others as others now are unto her."

"Never fear," answered Poor Turkey Girl. "In everything you direct me to do I shall be obedient, as you have always been to me."

When the sun had just begun to set, the turkeys turned homeward of their own accord and the maiden followed them, happy and light of heart. The old gobbler called to Poor Turkey Girl: "Enter our house. Sit down and give us your clothing. We shall try to renew it."

Obediently, Poor Turkey Girl drew off her ragged mantle and cast it on the ground. The old gobbler seized it in his beak, spread it out, and picked and picked at it. Then he trod upon it, strutting back and forth. Taking it up in his beak, he puffed and puffed at it, and then laid down at the feet of the maiden—a beautiful white embroidered cotton mantle.

A second gobbler came forth and Poor Turkey Girl gave him another piece of her clothing. Then another and another she handed over for their magic, until each garment she had worn was now new and as beautiful as any possessed by her mistresses in Mátsaki.

Before Turkey Girl arrayed herself in these handsome garments, the turkeys circled about her, singing and clucking and brushing her with their wings until she was clean and her skin as smooth and bright as that of the finest maiden in Mátsaki. Her hair became soft and wavy, instead of a sunburnt shock. Her cheeks appeared full and dimpled, and her eyes danced with smiles. She saw how true had been the turkeys' words.

Finally, one old turkey came forward. He said: "You lack now only the rich ornaments worn by those who have many possessions. But wait a moment. We turkeys have keen eyes and have gathered many valuable things lost by men and maidens." Spreading his wings, he trod round and round, throwing his head back. Presently he coughed and there in his beak was a beautiful necklace. Another turkey in the same way brought forth earrings, and on and on, until Poor Turkey Girl had all the proper ornaments, as many as she could wear.

She decorated herself with their beautiful ornaments and thanked the turkeys for all they had done for her. As she started to leave them, they called out: "Oh, maiden mother, you must leave the gate open for us. Who knows that you will remember your turkeys when your fortune changes. Will you not grow ashamed that you have been the maiden mother of turkeys? Know that we love you and wish for you good fortune, but remember our words and do not tarry too long."

Turkey Girl, who could no longer be called Poor Turkey Girl, sped away down the river path toward Zuñi, calling back: "I will remember, my turkeys!"

Through a long covered way she entered the town and went into the dance court. There when she appeared murmurs ran through the crowd—sounds of astonishment at her beauty and the richness of her dress. Everyone asked, "Whence comes this beautiful maiden?"

Not long did Turkey Girl stand neglected. The leaders of the dance, gorgeously decked in holiday attire, hastily

invited her to join the youths and maidens dancing around the musicians and the altar in the center of the plaza. With a blush and a smile and a toss of her hair over her eyes she willingly stepped into the circle, where her hand in dancing was quickly sought. Her heart became light and her feet merry, and she danced until the sun sank low in the west.

Alas! In her enjoyment Turkey Girl had not heeded the wishes of her turkeys as she had promised to do. She said only, to herself, "I shall stay just a little while longer. Before the sun sets, I shall run back to my turkeys, so that these people may not see who I am."

Time sped on, and another dance was called, and then another. Never for a moment did people let her rest, but drew her into each dance around the musicians and the altar in the center of the plaza.

At last the sun set and the dancing was nearly done. Suddenly, Turkey Girl broke away and, being more swift of foot than most of the villagers, she sped up the river path before anyone could follow.

Meanwhile, the turkeys began to wonder that their maiden mother had not returned. At last gray old gobbler exclaimed: "It is just as we might have expected. She has forgotten us. Let us go to the mountains and endure no more of this captivity. We can no longer think of our maiden mother to be as good and true as once we thought her."

Calling to one another in loud voices, they trooped out of their cages and ran toward the Cañon of the Cottonwoods, around Thunder Mountain, through the Gateway of Zuñi, and up into the valley.

Turkey Girl arrived at the open gate. Behold! Not one turkey! Trailing their course, she ran up the valley to overtake them. But they were now far ahead and it was a long time before she heard them singing this song:

Up the river, *to! to!*
Up the river, *to! to!*
    Sing *ye ye!*

81

Up the river, *to! to!*
Up the river, *to! to!*
    Sing *yee huli huli!*

Oh, our maiden mother
To the Middle Place
    To dance went away;
Therefore as she lingers,
To the Cañon Mesa
And the plains above it
    We all run away!
    Sing *ye yee huli huli,*
    Tot-tot, tot-tot, tot-tot,
    Huli huli!
    Tot-tot, tot-tot, tot-tot,
    Huli huli!

Hearing this, the maiden called to her turkeys. But she called and called in vain. They only spread their wings to quicken their flight, singing the song over and over until they came to the base of the Cañon Mesa, at the border of the Zuñi Mountains. Finally, now singing in full chorus, they fluttered away above the plains.

Turkey Girl threw up her hands. She looked down at her dress. Behold! It was now what it had been. She was Poor Turkey Girl as before. Weary, grieving, and despairing, she returned to Mátsaki.

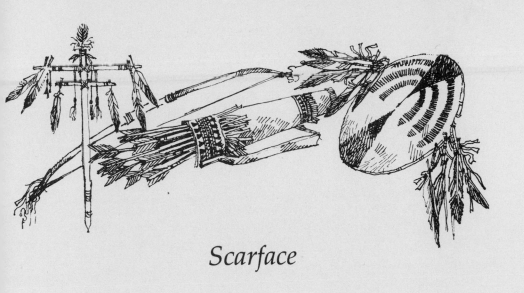

Scarface

In the earliest times there was a man who had a very beautiful daughter. Many young men wished to marry her, but whenever she was asked she shook her head and said she did not want a husband.

"Why is this?" said her father. "Some of these young men are rich, handsome, and brave."

"Why should I marry?" replied the girl. "My father and mother take care of me. Our lodge is good; the parfleches* are never empty; there are plenty of tanned robes and soft furs for winter. Why trouble me, then?"

Soon after, the Raven Bearers held a dance. They all painted themselves nicely and wore their finest ornaments and each one tried to dance the best. Afterward some of them asked for this girl, but she said "No." After that the Bulls, the Kit-Foxes, and others of the All Comrades held their dances, and many men who were rich and some great warriors asked this man for his daughter, but to every one she said, "No."

Then her father was angry, and he said, "Why is this? All

*Saddlebags of rawhide.

the best men have asked for you, and you still say 'No.' "
Then the girl said, "Father, listen to me. That Above Person, the Sun, said to me, 'Do not marry any of these men,
for you belong to me. Listen to what I say, and you shall be
happy and live to a great age.' And again he said to me,
'Take heed, you must not marry; you are mine.' "

"Ah!" replied her father, "it must always be as he says";
and they spoke no more about it.

There was a poor young man. He was very poor. His
father, his mother, and all his relations were dead. He had
no lodge, no wife to tan his robes or make his moccasins.
His clothes were always old and worn. He had no home.
To-day he stopped in one lodge; then to-morrow he ate
and slept in another. Thus he lived. He had a good face, but
on his cheek was a bad scar.

After they had held those dances, some of the young
men met this poor Scarface, and they laughed at him and
said, "Why do not you ask that girl to marry you? You are
so rich and handsome."

Scarface did not laugh. He looked at them and said, "I
will do as you say: I will go and ask her."

All the young men thought this was funny; they laughed
a good deal at Scarface as he was walking away.

Scarface went down by the river and waited there, near
the place where the women went to get water. By and by
the girl came there. Scarface spoke to her and said. "Girl,
stop: I want to speak with you. I do not wish to do anything
secretly, but I speak to you here openly, where the Sun
looks down and all may see."

"Speak, then," said the girl.

"I have seen the days," said Scarface. "I have seen how
you refused all those men, who are young and rich and
brave. To-day some of these young men laughed and said
to me, 'Why do not you ask her?' I am poor. I have no
lodge, no food, no clothes, no robes. I have no relations.
All of them have died. Yet now to-day I say to you, take
pity. Be my wife."

The girl hid her face in her robe and brushed the ground with the point of her moccasin, back and forth, back and forth, for she was thinking.

After a time she spoke and said, "It is true I have refused all those rich young men; yet now a poor one asks me, and I am glad. I will be your wife, and my people will be glad. You are poor but that does not matter. My father will give you dogs; my mother will make us a lodge; my relations will give us robes and furs; you will no longer be poor."

Then the young man was glad, and he started forward to kiss her, but she put out her hand and held him back, and said, "Wait; the Sun has spoken to me. He said I may not

85

marry; that I belong to him; that if I listen to him I shall live to great age. So now I say, go to the Sun; say to him, 'She whom you spoke with has listened to your words; she has never done wrong, but now she wants to marry. I want her for my wife.' Ask him to take that scar from your face; that will be his sign, and I shall know he is pleased. But if he refuses, or if you cannot find his lodge, then do not return to me."

"Oh!" cried Scarface; "at first your words were good. I was glad. But now it is dark. My heart is dead. Where is that far-off lodge? Where is the trail that no one yet has travelled?"

"Take courage, take courage," said the girl softly, and she went on to her lodge.

Scarface was very unhappy. He did not know what to do. He sat down and covered his face with his robe, and tried to think. At length he stood up and went to an old woman who had been kind to him, and said to her, "Pity me. I am poor. I am going away, on a long journey. Make me some moccasins."

"Where are you going—far from the camp?" asked the old woman.

"I do not know where I am going," he replied; "I am in trouble, but I cannot talk about it."

This old woman had a kind heart. She made him moccasins—seven pairs; and gave him also a sack of food— pemmican, dried meat, and back fat.

All alone and with a sad heart, Scarface climbed the bluff that overlooked the valley, and when he reached the top, turned to look back at the camp. He wondered if he should ever see it again; if he should return to the girl and to the people.

"Pity me, O Sun!" he prayed; and turning away, he set off to look for the trail to the Sun's lodge.

For many days he went on. He crossed great prairies and followed up timbered rivers, and crossed the mountains. Every day his sack of food grew lighter, but as he went along he looked for berries and roots, and sometimes he killed an animal. These things gave him food.

One night he came to the home of a wolf. "Hah!" said the wolf; "what are you doing so far from your home?"

"I am looking for the place where the Sun lives," replied Scarface. "I have been sent to speak with him."

"I have travelled over much country," said the wolf; "I know all the prairies, the valleys, and the mountains; but I have never seen the Sun's home. But wait a moment. I know a person who is very wise, and who may be able to tell you the road. Ask the bear."

The next day Scarface went on again, stopping now and then to rest and pick berries, and when night came he was at the bear's lodge.

"Where is your home?" asked the bear. "Why are you travelling so far alone?"

"Ah," replied the man, "I have come to you for help. Pity me. Because of what that girl said to me, I am looking for the Sun. I wish to ask him for her."

"I do not know where he lives," said the bear. "I have travelled by many rivers and I know the mountains, yet I have not seen his lodge. Farther on there is some one—that striped face—who knows a great deal; ask him."

When the young man got there, the badger was in his hole. But Scarface called to him, "Oh, cunning striped face! I wish to speak with you."

The badger put his head out of the hole and said, "What do you want, my brother?"

"I wish to find the Sun's home," said Scarface. "I wish to speak with him."

"I do not know where he lives," answered the badger. "I never travel very far. Over there in the timber is the wolverene. He is always travelling about, and knows many things. Perhaps he can tell you."

Scarface went over to the forest and looked all about for the wolverene, but could not see him; so he sat on a log to rest. "Alas, alas!" he cried; "wolverene, take pity on me.

My food is gone, my moccasins are worn out; I fear I shall die."

Some one close to him said, "What is it, my brother?" and looking around, he saw the wolverene sitting there.

"She whom I wish to marry belongs to the Sun," said Scarface; "I am trying to find where he lives, so that I may ask him for her."

"Ah," said the wolverene, "I know where he lives. It is nearly night now, but tomorrow I will show you the trail to the big water. He lives on the other side of it."

Early in the morning they set out, and the wolverene showed Scarface the trail, and he followed it until he came to the water's edge. When he looked out over it, his heart almost stopped. Never before had any one seen such a great water. The other side could not be seen and there was no end to it. Scarface sat down on the shore. This seemed the end. His food was gone; his moccasins were worn out; he had no longer strength, no longer courage; his heart was sick. "I cannot cross this great water," he said. "I cannot return to the people. Here by this water I shall die."

Yet, even as he thought this, helpers were near. Two swans came swimming up to the shore and said to him, "Why have you come here? What are you doing? It is very far to the place where your people live."

"I have come here to die," replied Scarface. "Far away in my country is a beautiful girl. I want to marry her, but she belongs to the Sun; so I set out to find him and ask him for her. I have travelled many days. My food is gone. I cannot go back; I cannot cross this great water; so I must die."

"No," said the swans; "it shall not be so. Across this water is the home of that Above Person. Get on our backs, and we will take you there."

Scarface stood up. Now he felt strong and full of courage. He waded out into the water and lay down on the swans' backs, and they swam away. It was a fearful journey, for that water was deep and black, and in it lived strange people and great animals which might reach up and seize a person and pull him down under the water; yet the swans carried Scarface safely to the other side. There was seen a broad hard trail leading back from the water's edge.

"There," said the swans; "you are now close to the Sun's lodge. Follow that trail, and soon you will see it."

Scarface started to walk along the trail, and after he had gone a little way he came to some beautiful things lying in the trail. There was a war shirt, a shield, a bow, and a quiver of arrows. He had never seen such fine weapons. He looked at them, but he did not touch them, and at last walked around them and went on. A little farther along he met a young man, a very handsome person. His hair was long; his clothing was made of strange skins, and his moccasins were sewed with bright feathers.

The young man spoke to him and asked, "Did you see some weapons lying in the trail?"

"Yes," said Scarface, "I saw them."

"Did you touch them?" said the young man.

"No," said Scarface; "I supposed some one had left them there, and I did not touch them."

"You do not meddle with the property of others," said the young man. "What is your name, and where are you going?" Scarface told him. Then said the young man, "My name is Early Riser (the morning star). The Sun is my father. Come, I will take you to our lodge. My father is not at home now, but he will return at night."

At length they came to the lodge. It was large and handsome, and on it were painted strange medicinal animals. On a tripod behind the lodge were the Sun's weapons and his war clothing. Scarface was ashamed to go into the lodge, but Morning Star said, "Friend, do not be afraid; we are glad you have come."

When they went in a woman was sitting there, the Moon, the Sun's wife and the mother of Morning Star. She spoke to Scarface kindly and gave him food to eat, and when he had eaten she asked, "Why have you come so far from your people?"

So Scarface told her about the beautiful girl that he wished to marry and said, "She belongs to the Sun. I have come to ask him for her."

When it was almost night, and time for the Sun to come home, the Moon hid Scarface under a pile of robes. As soon as the Sun got to the doorway he said, "A strange person is here."

"Yes, father," said Morning Star, "a young man has come to see you. He is a good young man, for he found some of my things in the trail and did not touch them."

Scarface came out from under the robes and the Sun entered the lodge and sat down. He spoke to Scarface and said, "I am glad you have come to our lodge. Stay with us as long as you like. Sometimes my son is lonely. Be his friend."

The next day the two young men were talking about going hunting and the Moon spoke to Scarface and said, "Go with my son where you like, but do not hunt near that big water. Do not let him go there. That is the home of great birds with long, sharp bills. They kill people. I have had many sons, but these birds have killed them all. Only Morning Star is left."

Scarface stayed a long time in the Sun's lodge, and every day went hunting with Morning Star. One day they came near the water and saw the big birds.

"Come on," said Morning Star, "let us go and kill those birds."

"No, no," said Scarface, "we must not go there. Those are terrible birds; they will kill us."

Morning Star would not listen. He ran toward the water and Scarface ran after him, for he knew that he must kill the birds and save the boy's life. He ran ahead of Morning Star and met the birds, which were coming to fight, and killed every one of them with his spear; not one was left. The young men cut off the heads of the birds and carried them home, and when Morning Star's mother heard what they had done, and they showed her the birds' heads, she was glad. She cried over the two young men and called Scarface "My son," and when the Sun came home at night she told him about it, and he too was glad.

"My son," he said to Scarface, "I will not forget what you have this day done for me. Tell me now what I can do for you; what is your trouble?"

"Alas, alas!" replied Scarface, "Pity me. I came here to ask you for that girl. I want to marry her. I asked her and she was glad, but she says that she belongs to you, and that you told her not to marry."

"What you say is true," replied the Sun. "I have seen the days and all that she has done. Now I give her to you. She is yours. I am glad she has been wise, and I know that she has never done wrong. The Sun takes care of good women; they shall live a long time and so shall their husbands and children.

"Now, soon you will go home. I wish to tell you something and you must be wise and listen. I am the only chief; everything is mine; I made the earth, the mountains, the prairies, the rivers, and the forests; I made the people and all the animals. This is why I say that I alone am chief. I can never die. It is true the winter makes me old and weak, but every summer I grow young again.

"What one of all the animals is the smartest?" the Sun went on. "It is the raven, for he always finds food; he is never hungry. Which one of all the animals is the most to be reverenced? It is the buffalo; of all the animals I like him best. He is for the people; he is your food and your shelter. What part of his body is sacred? It is the tongue; that belongs to me. What else is sacred? Berries. They too are mine. Come with me now and see the world."

The Sun took Scarface to the edge of the sky and they looked down and saw the world. It is flat and round, and all around the edge it goes straight down. Then said the Sun, "If any man is sick or in danger his wife may promise to build me a lodge if he recovers. If the woman is good, then I shall be pleased and help the man; but if she is not good, or if she lies, then I shall be angry. You shall build the lodge like the world, round, with walls, but first you must build a sweat-lodge of one hundred sticks. It shall be arched like the sky, and one-half of it shall be painted red for me, the other half you shall paint black for the night." He told Scarface all about making the Medicine Lodge, and when he had finished speaking, he rubbed some medicine on the young man's face and the scar that had been there disappeared. He gave him two raven feathers, saying: "These are a sign for the girl that I give her to you. They must always be worn by the husband of the woman who builds a Medicine Lodge."

Now Scarface was ready to return home. The Sun and Morning Star gave him many good presents; the Moon cried and kissed him and was sorry to see him go. Then the Sun showed him the short trail. It was the Wolf Road—the Milky Way. He followed it and soon reached the ground.

It was a very hot day. All the lodge skins were raised and the people sat in the shade. There was a chief, a very generous man, who all day long was calling out for feasts, and people kept coming to his lodge to eat and smoke with him. Early in the morning this chief saw sitting on a butte* near by a person close-wrapped in his robe. All day long this person sat there and did not move. When it was almost night the chief said, "That person has sat there all day in the strong heat, and has not eaten nor drunk. Perhaps he is a stranger. Go and ask him to come to my lodge."

Some young men ran up to the person and said to him, "Why have you sat here all day in the great heat? Come to the shade of the lodges. The chief asks you to eat with him." The person rose and threw off his robe and the young men were surprised. He wore fine clothing; his

*Steep hill.

92

bow, shield, and other weapons were of strange make; but they knew his face, although the scar was gone, and they ran ahead, shouting, "The Scarface poor young man has come. He is poor no longer. The scar on his face is gone."

All the people hurried out to see him and to ask him questions. "Where did you get all these fine things?" He did not answer. There in the crowd stood that young woman, and, taking the two raven feathers from his head, he gave them to her and said, "The trail was long and I nearly died, but by those helpers I found his lodge. He is glad. He sends these feathers to you. They are the sign."

Great was her gladness then. They were married and made the first Medicine Lodge, as the Sun had said. The Sun was glad. He gave them great age. They were never sick. When they were very old, one morning their children called to them, "Awake, rise and eat." They did not move.

In the night, together, in sleep, without pain, their shadows had departed to the Sandhills.

The Indian Cinderella

On the shores of a wide bay on the Atlantic coast there dwelt in old times a great Indian warrior. It was said that he had been one of Glooskap's best helpers and friends and that he had done for him many wonderful deeds. But that, no man knows. He had, however, a very wonderful and strange power: he could make himself invisible; he could thus mingle unseen with his enemies and listen to their plots. He was known among the people as Strong Wind the Invisible. He dwelt with his sister in a tent near the sea, and his sister helped him greatly in his work. Many maidens would have been glad to marry him, and he was much sought-after because of his mighty deeds; and it was known that Strong Wind would marry the first maiden who could see him as he came home at night. Many made the trial, but it was a long time before one succeeded.

Strong Wind used a clever trick to test the truthfulness of all who sought to win him. Each evening, as the day went down, his sister walked on the beach with any girl who wished to make the trial. His sister could always see him, but no one else could see him. And as he came home from work in the twilight, his sister, as she saw him drawing

94

near, would ask the girl who sought him: "Do you see him?" And each girl would falsely answer: "Yes." And his sister would ask: "With what does he draw his sled?" And each girl would answer: "With the hide of a moose," or "With a pole," or "With a great cord." And then his sister would know that they all had lied, for their answers were mere guesses. And many tried and lied and failed, for Strong Wind would not marry any who were untruthful.

There lived in the village a great Chief who had three daughters. Their mother had long been dead. One of these was much younger than the others. She was very beautiful and gentle and well beloved by all, and for that reason her older sisters were very jealous of her charms and treated her very cruelly. They clothed her in rags that she might be ugly, and they cut off her long black hair, and they burned her face with coals from the fire that she might be scarred and disfigured. And they lied to their father, telling him that she had done these things herself. But the young girl was patient and kept her gentle heart and went gladly about her work.

Like other girls, the Chief's two oldest daughters tried to win Strong Wind. One evening, as the day went down, they walked on the shore with Strong Wind's sister and waited for his coming. Soon he came home from his day's work, drawing his sled. And his sister asked as usual: "Do you see him?" and each one, lying, answered: "Yes." And she asked: "Of what is his shoulder-strap made?" And each guessing, said: "Of rawhide." Then they entered the tent, where they hoped to see Strong Wind eating his supper, and when he took off his coat and his moccasins they could see them, but more than these they saw nothing. And Strong Wind knew that they had lied, and he kept himself from their sight, and they went home dismayed.

One day the Chief's youngest daughter with her rags and her burnt face resolved to seek Strong Wind. She patched her clothes with bits of birch bark from the trees and put on the few little ornaments she possessed and

95

went forth to try to see the Invisible One as all the other girls of the village had done before. And her sisters laughed at her and called her "Fool'; and as she passed along the road, all the people laughed at her because of her tattered frock and her burnt face, but silently she went her way.

Strong Wind's sister received the little girl kindly, and at twilight she took her to the beach. Soon Strong Wind came home drawing his sled. And his sister asked: "Do you see him?" And the girl answered: "No"; and his sister wondered greatly because she spoke the truth. And again she asked: "Do you see him now?" And the girl answered: "Yes, and he is very wonderful." And she asked: "With what does he draw his sled?" And the girl answered: "With the Rainbow," and she was much afraid. And she asked further: "Of what is his bow-string?" And the girl answered: "His bow-string is the Milky Way."

Then Strong Wind's sister knew that because the girl had spoken the truth at first, her brother had made himself visible to her. And she said: "Truly, you have seen him." And she took her home and bathed her, and all the scars disappeared from her face and body; and her hair grew long and black again like the raven's wing; and she gave her fine clothes to wear and many rich ornaments. Then she bade her take the wife's seat in the tent. Soon Strong Wind entered and sat beside her and called her his bride. The very next day she became his wife, and ever afterwards she helped him to do great deeds. The girl's two elder sisters were very cross and they wondered greatly at what had taken place. But Strong Wind, who knew of their cruelty, resolved to punish them. Using his great power, he changed them both into aspen trees and rooted them in the earth. And since that day the leaves of the aspen have always trembled, and they shiver in fear at the approach of Strong Wind, it matters not how softly he comes, for they are still mindful of his great power and anger because of their lies and their cruelty to their sister long ago.

Star Maiden

Waupee the White Hawk lived in a deep forest where animals and birds were abundant. Each day he returned from the chase well rewarded, for he was one of the most skillful hunters of his tribe. No part of the forest was too dark for him to penetrate, and there was no track he could not follow.

One day he went beyond any point he had visited before, through an open bit of forest which enabled him to see a great distance. Light breaking through showed that he was on the edge of a wide plain covered with grass. He walked here for some time without a path, then suddenly came to a ring worn down in the earth as if made by footsteps following a circle. What excited him was the fact that there was no path leading into the ring or away from it. He could find no trace of footsteps in any crushed leaf or broken twig.

Waupee thought he would hide and watch to see, if he could, what had made the circle. Very soon he heard faint sounds of music. He looked up and saw a small something descending to earth. From a mere speck it grew bigger and

97

the music became stronger and sweeter. He beheld a basket in which rode twelve beautiful maidens.

As soon as the basket touched the ground, the girls leaped out. They began to dance round the magic ring, striking a shining ball as they flitted past. Waupee gazed upon their graceful movements. He admired them all, but most of all the youngest. Unable to restrain his admiration, suddenly he rushed out of his hiding place and tried to seize her. But the sisters, quick as birds, as soon as they saw him leaped into the basket and rose up into the sky.

Waupee gazed till he could see them no more. "They are gone, and I shall not see them again," he sighed. Filled with a deep sadness he returned to his lonely lodge. His mind could not rest. Hunting, his favorite sport, he could no longer enjoy, nor the companionship around the fire at night with the storytellers, nor the admiration of the girls of his tribe.

The next day Waupee returned to the prairie to wait near the ring. This time, in order to deceive the sisters, he assumed the form of an opossum. The basket again floated down, to the center of the magic ring, and once more he heard the sweet music. The maidens leaped out and began their sportive dancing. They seemed to Waupee to be even more beautiful and graceful this time.

In his disguise, Waupee crept slowly through the grass towards the ring, but the instant he appeared, ready to seize the youngest, the sisters sprang together into their basket. It rose, but when it was only a short distance off the ground, Waupee heard one of the older girls speak. "Perhaps," she said, "it came to show us how our game is played on earth."

"Oh, no!" replied the youngest, "Quick, let us ascend."

Once more the basket floated upward out of sight.

Waupee returned to his own form and walked sorrowfully back to his lodge. The night seemed long, and back to the plain he went early the next day. How could he secure that lovely maiden? While he pondered, he noticed an old stump of a tree near by in which mice were running about. He brought the stump over near the ring. "So small a creature would not cause alarm," he thought, and thereupon he turned himself into a mouse.

The sisters floated down and took up their game. "But, look," cried the youngest. "That stump was not there yesterday." Frightened, she ran to the basket. The others, however, only smiled and gathered around it. When they struck at it playfully, the mice ran out, Waupee among them. The girls killed all but one, which was pursued by the youngest sister. Just as she raised her stick to kill it, Waupee rose and clasped her in his arms. Her eleven sisters sprang quickly into their basket and rose up into the sky.

Waupee displayed all his skills, to please his bride and win her affection. As he wiped away her tears, he praised the way of life on earth. He was determined to make her forget her sisters. From the moment she entered his lodge with him, he was one of the happiest of men.

Winter and summer passed away and the girl found she loved this young hunter. Their happiness was greater when a beautiful boy was born to them.

But Waupee's wife was a daughter of one of the stars and she longed to visit her old home. While Waupee was hunting she managed to make a wicker basket, secretly, in the middle of the magic ring.

When it was finished she collected rarities, including special foods from earth, to please her father. With these she went one day when Waupee was away, taking her little son with her into the charmed ring. As soon as they had climbed into the basket, she began to sing and the basket rose.

The wind carried her song to her husband's ear. He recognized her voice and ran at once to the prairie. But he could not reach the ring before his wife and child were ascending. He called and called after them, but they did not heed his appeals. Waupee could only watch the basket until it was a small speck and finally vanished in the sky. In utter grief, he lay down on the ground.

Through a long winter and a long summer, Waupee bewailed his loss and could find no relief. He mourned for his wife and even more for his son.

In the meantime Waupee's wife had reached her home among the stars and almost forgot that she had left a husband on earth. The presence of her son reminded her, however, for as he grew up he began to wish to visit his father. One day his grandfather, who was the Star Chief, said to his daughter, "Go, take your son to see his father, and ask him to come to live with us. Tell him to bring with him one of each kind of bird and animal he kills in the chase."

Accordingly, Waupee's wife took the boy and descended to earth. Waupee, who was never far from the enchanted circle, heard her voice as she came down from the sky. His heart beat with impatience as he saw her and his son, and he soon had them in his arms.

His wife gave him her father's message and Waupee began at once to hunt. Whole nights as well as days he searched for every beautiful or curiously different bird and animal. He took only a tail, foot, or wing— enough to identify each. When all was ready, he went with his wife and child to the circle and they floated up.

Great joy greeted their arrival in the starry world. The Star Chief invited all his people to a feast. When they were together, he announced that each might take one of the earthly gifts, whichever was most admired. Some chose a foot, some a wing, some a tail, and some a claw. Those who selected a tail or claw became animals and ran off. The others assumed the form of birds and flew away. Waupee chose a white hawk's feather and his wife and son followed his example. All three now became white hawks and spread their great wings. They descended with the other birds down to earth, where they may still be found.

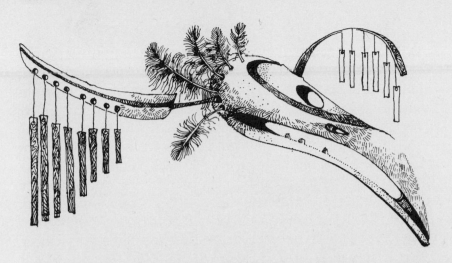

The Blessed Gift of Joy is Bestowed Upon Man

Once there was a time when men knew no joy. Their whole life was work, food, digestion, and sleep. One day went by like another. They toiled, they slept, they awoke again to toil. Monotony rusted their minds.

In these days there was a man and his wife who lived alone in their dwelling not far from the sea. They had three sons, all spirited lads, anxious to be as good huntsmen as their father, and even before they were full grown they entered into all kinds of activities to make them strong and enduring. And their father and mother felt proud and secure in the thought that the boys would provide for their old age and find them food when they could no longer help themselves.

But it happened that the eldest son, and after a while the second one, went a-hunting and never came back. They left no trace behind; all search was in vain. And the father and mother grieved deeply over their loss and watched now with great anxiety over the youngest boy, who was at this time big enough to accompany his father when he went hunting. The son, who was called Ermine (Teriak) liked best to stalk caribou, whereas his father preferred to hunt sea creatures. And, as hunters cannot spend all their lives in anxiety, it soon came about that the son was allowed to go where he pleased inland while the father rowed to sea in his kayak.

One day, stalking caribou as usual, Ermine suddenly caught sight of a mighty eagle, a big young eagle that circled over him. Ermine pulled out his arrows, but did not shoot as the eagle flew down and settled on the ground a short distance from him. Here it took off its hood and became a young man who said to the boy:

"It was I who killed your two brothers. I will kill you too unless you promise to hold a festival of song when you get home. Will you or won't you?"

"Gladly, but I don't understand what you say. What is song? What is a festival?"

"Will you or won't you?"

"Gladly, but I don't know what it is."

"If you follow me my mother will teach you what you don't understand. Your two brothers scorned the gifts of song and merrymaking; they would not learn, so I killed them. Now you may come with me, and as soon as you have learned to put words together into a song and to sing it—as soon as you have learned to dance for joy, you shall be free to go home to your dwelling."

"I'll come with you," answered Ermine. And off they set.

The eagle was no longer a bird but a big strong man in a gleaming cloak of eagles' feathers. They walked and they walked, farther and farther inland, through gorges and valleys, onward to a high mountain, which they began to climb.

"High up on that mountain top stands our house," said the young eagle. And they clambered on over the mountain, up and up until they had a wide view over the plains of the caribou hunters.

102

But as they approached the crest of the mountain, they suddenly heard a throbbing sound, which grew louder and louder the nearer they came to the top. It sounded like the strokes of huge hammers, and so loud was the noise that it set Ermine's ears a-humming.

"Do you hear anything?" asked the eagle.

"Yes, a strange deafening noise, that isn't like anything I've ever heard before."

"It is the beating of my mother's heart," answered the eagle.

So they approached the eagle's house, that was built right on the uttermost peaks.

"Wait here until I come back. I must prepare my mother," said the eagle, and went in.

A moment after, he came back and fetched Ermine. They entered a big room, fashioned like the dwellings of men, and on the bunk, quite alone, sat the eagle's mother, aged, feeble, and sad. Her son now said:

"Here's a man who has promised to hold a song festival when he gets home. But he says men don't understand how to put words together into songs, nor even how to beat drums and dance for joy. Mother, men don't know how to make merry, and now this young man has come up here to learn."

This speech brought fresh life to the feeble old mother eagle, and her tired eyes lit up suddenly while she said:

"First you must build a feast hall where many men may gather."

So the two young men set to work and built the feast hall, which is called a *kagsse* and is larger and finer than ordinary houses. And when it was finished the mother eagle taught them to put words together into songs and to add tones to the words so that they could be sung. She made a drum and taught them to beat upon it in rhythm with the music, and she showed them how they should dance to the songs. When Ermine had learned all this she said:

103

"Before every festival you must collect much meat, and then call together many men. This you must do after you have built your feast hall and made your songs. For when men assemble for a festival they require sumptuous meals."

"But we know of no men but ourselves," answered Ermine.

"Men are lonely, because they have not yet received the gift of joy," said the mother eagle. "Make all your preparations as I have told you. When all is ready you shall go out and seek for men. You will meet them in couples. Gather them until they are many in number and invite them to come with you. Then hold your festival of song."

Thus spoke the old mother eagle, and when she had minutely instructed Ermine in what he should do, she finally said to him:

"I may be an eagle, yet I am also an aged woman with the same pleasures as other women. A gift calls for a return, therefore it is only fitting that in farewell you should give me a little sinew string. It will be but a slight return, yet it will give me pleasure."

Ermine was at first miserable, for wherever was he to procure sinew string so far from his home? But suddenly he remembered that his arrow-heads were lashed to the shafts with sinew string. He unwound these and gave the string to the eagle. Thus was his return gift only a trifling matter. Thereupon, the young eagle again drew on his shining cloak and bade his guest bestride his back and put his arms round his neck. Then he threw himself out over the mountainside. A roaring sound was heard around them and Ermine thought his last hour had come. But this lasted only a moment; then the eagle halted and bade him open his eyes. And there they were again at the place where they had met. They had become friends and now they must part, and they bade each other a cordial farewell. Ermine hastened home to his parents and related all his adventures to them, and he concluded his narrative with these words:

"Men are lonely; they live without joy because they don't know how to make merry. Now the eagle has given me the blessed gift of rejoicing, and I have promised to invite all men to share in the gift."

Father and mother listened in surprise to the son's tale and shook their heads incredulously, for he who has never felt his blood glow and his heart throb in exultation cannot imagine such a gift as the eagle's. But the old people dared not gainsay him, for the eagle had already taken two of their sons, and they understood that its word had to be obeyed if they were to keep this last child. So they did all that the eagle had required of them.

A feast hall, matching the eagles', was built, and the larder was filled with the meat of sea creatures and caribou. Father and son combined joyous words, describing their dearest and deepest memories in songs which they set to music; also they made drums, rumbling tambourines of taut caribou hides with round wooden frames; and to the rhythm of the drum beats that accompanied the songs they moved their arms and legs in frolicsome hops and lively antics. Thus they grew warm both in mind and body, and began to regard everything about them in quite a new light. Many an evening it would happen that they joked and laughed, flippant and full of fun, at a time when they would otherwise have snored with sheer boredom the whole evening through.

As soon as all the preparations were made, Ermine went out to invite people to the festival that was to be held. To his great surprise he discovered that he and his parents were no longer alone as before. Merry men find company. Suddenly he met people everywhere, always in couples, strange-looking people, some clad in wolfskins, others in the fur of the wolverine, the lynx, the red fox, the silver fox, the cross fox—in fact, in the skins of all kinds of animals. Ermine invited them to the banquet in his new feast hall

105

and they all followed him joyfully. Then they held their song festival, each producing his own songs. There were laughter, talk, and sound, and people were carefree and happy as they had never been before. The table-delicacies were appreciated, gifts of meat were exchanged, friendships were formed, and there were several who gave each other costly gifts of fur. The night passed, and not till the morning light shone into the feast hall did the guests take their leave. Then, as they thronged out of the corridor, they all fell forward on their hands and sprang away on all fours. They were no longer men but had changed into wolves, wolverines, lynxes, silver foxes, red foxes—in fact, into all the beasts of the forest. They were the guests that the old eagle had sent, so that father and son might not seek in vain. So great was the power of joy that it could even change animals into men. Thus animals, who have always been more light-hearted than men, were man's first guests in a feast hall.

A little time after this it chanced that Ermine went hunting and again met the eagle. Immediately it took off its hood and turned into a man, and together they went up to the eagle's home, for the old mother eagle wanted once more to see the man who had held the first song festival for humanity.

Before they had reached the heights, the mother eagle came to thank them, and lo! the feeble old eagle had grown young again.

For when men make merry, all old eagles become young.

The foregoing is related by the old folk from Kanglanek, the land which lies where the forests begin around the source of Colville River. In this strange and unaccountable way, so they say, came to men the gift of joy.

And the eagle became the sacred bird of song, dance and all festivity.

Black American Tales

The Tar Baby

Once upon a time there was a water famine, and the runs went dry and the creeks went dry and the rivers went dry, and there wasn't any water to be found anywhere, so all the animals in the forest met together to see what could be done about it. The lion and the bear and the wolf and the fox and the giraffe and the monkey and elephant, and even the rabbit—everybody who lived in the forest was there, and they all tried to think of some plan by which they could get water. At last they decided to dig a well, and everybody said he would help—all except the rabbit, who always was a lazy little rascal, and he said he wouldn't dig. So the animals all said, "Very well, Mr. Rabbit, if you won't help dig this well, you shan't have one drop of water to drink." But the rabbit just laughed and said, as smart as you please, "Never mind, you dig the well and I'll get a drink all right."

Now the animals all worked very hard, all except the rabbit, and soon they had the well so deep that they struck water and they all got a drink and went away to their homes in the forest. But the very next morning what should they find but the rabbit's footprints in the mud at the mouth of the well, and they knew he had come in the night and stolen some water. So they all began to think how they could keep that lazy little rabbit from getting a drink, and they all talked and talked and talked, and after a while they decided that someone must watch the well, but no one seemed to want to stay up to do it. Finally, the bear said, "I'll watch the well the first night. You just go to bed, and I'll show old Mr. Rabbit that he won't get any water while I'm around."

So all the animals went away and left him, and the bear sat down by the well. By and by the rabbit came out of the thicket on the hillside and there he saw the old bear guarding the well. At first he didn't know what to do. Then he sat down and began to sing:

> *"Cha ra ra, will you, will you, can you?*
> *Cha ra ra, will you, will you, can you?"*

Presently the old bear lifted up his head and looked around. "Where's all that pretty music coming from?" he said. The rabbit kept on singing:

> *"Cha ra ra, will you, will you, can you?*
> *Cha ra ra, will you, will you, can you?"*

This time the bear got up on his hind feet. The rabbit kept on singing:

> *"Cha ra ra, will you, will you, can you?*
> *Cha ra ra, will you, will you, can you?"*

Then the bear began to dance, and after a while he danced so far away that the rabbit wasn't afraid of him any longer, and so he climbed down into the well and got a drink and ran away into the thicket.

Now when the animals came the next morning and found the rabbit's footprints in the mud, they made all kinds of fun of old Mr. Bear. They said, "Mr. Bear, you are a fine person to watch a well. Why, even Mr. Rabbit can outwit you." But the bear said, "The rabbit had nothing to do with it. I was sitting here wide-awake, when suddenly the most beautiful music came right down out of the sky. At least I think it came down out of the sky, for when I went to look for it, I could not find it, and it must have been while I was gone that Mr. Rabbit stole the water." "Anyway," said the other animals, "we can't trust you any more. Mr. Monkey, you had better watch the well tonight, and mind you, you'd better be pretty careful or old Mr. Rabbit will fool you." "I'd like to see him do it," said the monkey. "Just let him try." So the animals set the monkey to watch the well.

Presently it grew dark, and all the stars came out; and then the rabbit slipped out of the thicket and peeped over in the direction of the well. There he saw the monkey. Then he sat down on the hillside and began to sing:

> *"Cha ra ra, will you, will you, can you?*
> *Cha ra ra, will you, will you, can you?"*

Then the monkey peered down into the well. "It isn't the water," said he. The rabbit kept on singing:

> *"Cha ra ra, will you, will you, can you?*
> *Cha ra ra, will you, will you, can you?"*

This time the monkey looked into the sky. "It isn't the stars," said he. The rabbit kept on singing.

This time the monkey looked toward the forest. "It must be the leaves," said he. "Anyway, it's too good music to let go to waste." So he began to dance, and after a while he danced so far away that the rabbit wasn't afraid, so he climbed down into the well and got a drink and ran off into the thicket.

Well, the next morning, when all the animals came down and found the footprints again, you should have heard them talk to that monkey. They said, "Mr. Monkey, you are no better than Mr. Bear; neither of you is of any account. You can't catch a rabbit." And the monkey said, "It wasn't old Mr. Rabbit's fault at all that I left the well. He

111

had nothing to do with it. All at once the most beautiful music that you ever heard came out of the woods, and I went to see who was making it." But the animals only laughed at him. Then they tried to get someone else to watch the well that night. No one would do it. So they thought and thought and thought about what to do next. Finally the fox spoke up. "I'll tell you what let's do," said he. "Let's make a tar man and set him to watch the well." "Let's do," said the other animals together. So they worked the whole day long building a tar man and set him to watch the well.

That night the rabbit crept out of the thicket, and there he saw the tar man. So he sat down on the hillside and began to sing:

> "Cha ra ra, will you, will you, can you?
> Cha ra ra, will you, will you, can you?"

But the man never heard. The rabbit kept on singing:

> "Cha ra ra, will you, will you, can you?
> Cha ra ra, will you, will you, can you?"

The tar man never spoke. The rabbit came a little closer yet:

> "Cha ra ra, will you, will you, can you?
> Cha ra ra, will you, will you, can you?"

The tar man never spoke a word.

The rabbit came up close to the tar man. "Look here," he said, "you get out of my way and let me down into that well." The tar man never moved. "If you don't get out of my way, I'll hit you with my fist," said the rabbit. The tar man never moved a finger. Then the rabbit raised his fist and struck the tar man as hard as he could, and his right fist stuck tight in the tar. "Now you let go of my fist or I'll hit you with my other fist," said the rabbit. The tar man never budged. Then the rabbit struck him with his left fist, and his left fist stuck tight in the tar. "Now you let go of my fists or I'll kick you with my foot," said the rabbit. The tar man

112

never budged an inch. Then the rabbit kicked him with his right foot, and his right foot stuck tight in the tar. "Now you let go of my foot or I'll kick you with my other foot," said the rabbit. The tar man never stirred. Then the rabbit kicked him with his left foot, and his left foot stuck tight in the tar. "Now you let me go or I'll butt you with my head," said the rabbit. And he butted him with his head, and there he was; and there the other animals found him the next morning.

Well, you should have heard those animals laugh. "Oh, ho, Mr. Rabbit," they said. "Now we'll see whether you steal any more of our water or not. We're going to lay you across a log and cut your head off." "Oh, please do," said the rabbit. "I've always wanted to have my head cut off. I'd rather die that way than any other way I know." "Then we won't do it," said the other animals. "We are not going to kill you any way you like. We are going to shoot you." "That's better," said the rabbit. "If I had just stopped to think, I'd have asked you to do that in the first place. Please shoot me." "No, we'll not shoot you," said the other animals; and they had to think and think for a long time.

"I'll tell you what we'll do," said the bear. "We'll put you into a cupboard and let you eat and eat and eat until you are as fat as butter and then we'll throw you up into the air and let you come down and burst." "Oh, please don't!" said the rabbit. "I never wanted to die that way. Just do anything else, but please don't burst me." "Then that's exactly what we'll do," said all the other animals together.

So they put the rabbit into the cupboard and they fed him pie and cake and sugar, everything that was good; and by and by he got just as fat as butter. And then they took him out on the hillside and the lion took a paw, and the fox took a paw, and the bear took a paw, and the monkey took a paw; and then they swung him back and forth, and back and forth, saying: "One for the money, two for the show, three to make ready, and four to go." And they tossed him into the air, and he came down and lit on his feet and said:

"Yip, my name's Molly Cotton-tail;
Catch me if you can."

And off he ran into the thicket.

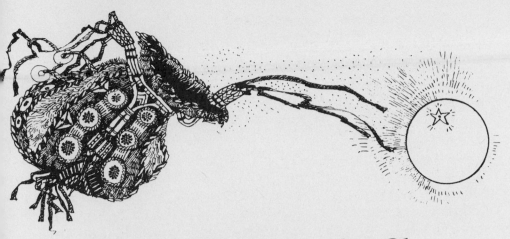

How Ole Woodpecker Got Ole Rabbit's Conjure Bag

One time, Old Woodpecker, he made up his mind that Old Rabbit was feeling too biggitty, and that the other creatures gave him lots of credit for smartness he didn't deserve. Woodpecker studied and studied this till he felt most distracted.

"How *am* I goin' to fetch Old Man Rabbit down?" he said to himself. "How *am* I going to make the creatures see that he ain't the man he sets himself up to be?"

That was the way he talked. And, he watched round Old Rabbit's place night and day, a-tryin' to fix him. He tried to conjure him, but that didn't work.

At last, when he was near worn out with a-studying, he made up his mind that he was goin' to steal Old Rabbit's conjure-bag. That would for sure take the importance out of Old Chuffy, because that bag, it was chock-full of luck-balls and herbs and balms, let alone the roots that could kill or cure just anything, and the big rabbit-foot that his mammy gave him. Oh, yes! that was a monstrous fine bag. It was full of everything I done told about, and besides that,

115

Conquer-John and may-apple that sprout in the dark of the moon and can talk in the dead of night, and jimson-burs and alanthus leaves that make fever and ague, and the grizzle-blue flowers that sprout where the dead snake lay and rot. Old Rabbit, he kept his fine silver ball there, too, when he was at home.

When Old Woodpecker studied about all these things, it fairly made his mouth drool. He made up his mind he was going to be neighborly with Old Rabbit, so he got into a good place and sang a friendly little song. When Old Chuffy noticed this, Old Woodpecker fetched him a little parcel of leaves off the top of the ash tree where Old Rabbit couldn't climb.

After that, Old Woodpecker dropped in, in the evenings, any time he had a mind to.

One time he dropped in when there was no one about except the little children and the old granny that was settin' asleep in the chimney corner. So Old Woodpecker talked might pretty to the children and gave them some clover to make them strong and some willow tops to make them gay. When they had eaten them, he fell to and asked them a heap of questions. At last, after asking about this and that and the other thing, he said—

"That be a mighty big, strong-lookin' box, yonder in the corner, the one with the big stone on top of it. It is like one I used to have but I don't have now. Maybe this is the same one. Let me see inside. If it is my old one, it has a mark in the lid that I cut there myself."

"Oh, no!" say they, "we dassent touch it. That's daddy's chest."

"What of that?" says Woodpecker, in a light manner as if he was poking fun. "If I look at that old box, you don't reckon I'm going to bore holes in it with my eyesight, do you?" says he, sort of easy and sort of sassy-like at the same time.

The children want to tell, but they ain't sure that their daddy won't be mad if they do. After they stand and grin for a while, the smallest one can't hold in no longer, and bursts out—

"That ain't no old box! That's where Daddy keeps his big conjure bag and all the truck that goes in the big kettle when the moon gets old."

That was just the news Old Woodpecker came for, but he don't get *all* the news he hoped for this trip, because Granny, she stretched and flinched like she was going to wake up, so off he went like a big devil was blowing behind him.

Granny wasn't asleeping like a rock, she caught a word or two, and, when she got her eyes open, she asked what had been going on.

The children felt out of sorts and would not tell. Never mind! Granny would catch them. That was all she asked now. She fetched supper.

The children couldn't eat.

She looked at them a long time. Sick? No, the children ain't sick. Conjured? No, they ain't conjured, because if they were, they'd holler when they go by the big chest. Uh-huh! They had something to eat and are ashamed to tell. Must have been Old Woodpecker brought it, because other neighbors would have stayed till Granny woke up. Uh-huh! the children are afraid they told something they ought to have kept. Uh-huh! They must have told about the conjure bag in the chest. Of course!

"*Children!*"

"W-wassa matter, G-Granny?"

"I wish Old Woodpecker'd drop in. He ain't been here for so long that I'm afeared the fuss you made the last time he came has run him off for good."

"Oh, no, Granny! He was here while you were a-sleepin'."

"I wish he'd stayed, because I done make him a little luck-ball for a present, but, shucks! He's such a big conjure-man himself, I don't expect he care for it after all."

"Oh, yes, Granny! Old Woodpecker does long for one.

He looked at the big chest that holds the conjure-bag just as if it was full of pumpkin-sass."

Now Granny caught them! My, she was mad! Because these children ain't minded their daddy. She whirled right at it and beat them with the clothes-line and sent them all to bed.

When Old Rabbit come home and heard that grand tale from the old granny he just tickled his ear with a straw and laughed. He unhitched the silver luck-ball from the string that held it under his arm and put it in the bag in the box along with the rest of the charms. Then he went to bed.

The next morning, he sent the family out visiting, and when they were gone he sat down and took a long time until the silver ball told him what to do.

That settled, he hid.

Pretty soon, along came Woodpecker, humming a little tune, to show that he was mighty gay and innocent.

He knocked on the door. "Ho there, folks!"

Nobody said anything.

He pushed the door open a crack. He peeked in. Nobody there? He flung the door wide open and went in.

"Uh-huh! Uh-huh! All out somewheres. This here's my chance. Now, Old Man Chuffy, I'm going to show you that Old Woodpecker is the biggest man at the hemp-breaking."

Old Woodpecker crossed the floor—tippetty, tip-petty—looking over his shoulder and jumping when a leaf fell down from the tree at the window.

By and by, he became more sassy feeling and he tried to get the big rock off the chest. No use. He couldn't do it. He pushed and he rolled and he heaved and he strained, until fire flashed from his eyeballs and his blood hummed in his ears. There it was, yet he couldn't budge it.

He sat back and cussed—when he had got breath enough.

"Sure! I'm going to cut a hole in the side of that box and fetch out the bag thataway!"

He cut a hole. It took him a long time, because that chest was made of mighty tough oak.

Shucks! When he reached in, there was another box, of ironwood.

Never mind! Cut again! Cut and cut and cut and cut. Land sakes, how tough the ironwood!

When he was almost ready to drop, he cut through. He reached for the bag. Jimminy squinch! He just caught hold of a little hickory box!

Then he cut and cut and cut and made a hole big enough in the two big boxes to get the little box out.

He was almost dead when he got that work done, but he tried to find the strength to carry that little box off to the woods.

When he got there he discovered that the box was bound up with hemp rope and the rope was conjured into tight knots. The knots he didn't untie: he cut them. Then he got to the bag and lifted it out. Ho! There now! There now!

That—bag—would—not—hold—still!

It wiggled and jounced around like a raccoon. He could scarcely hold it, so he got a big rope and tied it around it and then lashed it to a big tree, and I tell you that bag fought and scuffled until that tree squeaked and strained like it was getting pulled up.

Never mind! Old Woodpecker thought he would stop that. He piled some dry brush around that bag and set it afire. The fire burn high, burn bright, burn all red and yellow.

All of a sudden, the fire went down until there was just a blue ball.

Soon, from the middle of the ball came a voice—

"Woodpecker, put me back! Woodpecker, put me back!"

The next minute the silver luck-ball popped out and kept jumping, jumping towards Old Woodpecker. It scared Old Woodpecker so terribly that he forgot all the spells he knew.

119

"What are you after?" he mumbled as he backed away.

"Put me in the little chest," said the luck-ball.

Woodpecker took it up and put it in the chest, but it doesn't stay. It popped out and made for him again.

"Put me in the chest," hollered the ball.

"Ain't I put you in the chest and almost burned myself?" whimpered Woodpecker.

"Put me in the bag first, and then in the chest," said the luck-ball.

Woodpecker was a conjurer himself and he was bound to do that, though it burn him to the bone. He reached into the blue fire and grabbed that red-hot wolf bag and put the ball into it. Then he tied up the bag again. He had to tie it with conjure-knots and that was slow work. Then he dropped the awful mess into the chest.

The ball hollered out from the chest—

"Tie us up the way you found us."

Lands sake! He cut the rope into smidgins.

Never mind! He had to get hemp and twist another rope. After that he had to take the old rope and study the knots Old Rabbit tied in it.

All that time the burns were burning like the itch.

After a while, he got the knots tied. Then he took the box home.

"Mend this chest that you chopped," said the ball when Woodpecker put it where he found it.

He went back to the woods, he got oak and iron-wood and he mended the chests and carried off the chips.

Then the luck-ball say—

"I reckon you got your come-uppance, so I let you off easy this time. Just be comfortable. This is so little a matter that I ain't going to pester Old Rabbit with it. Go along home, now, and be done with this."

So Woodpecker go home. The burns were left so long that he could hardly conjure them at all. They were bad a long time and he had to keep mighty still.

After a while, when he got well and went out again, the first person he met up with was Old Chuffy, and Old Chuffy sort of grinned and twitched his nose and said—

"Hy-o! Neighbor, where you been this long time?"

Woodpecker, he grinned, but he couldn't say nothing.

The Conjure Wives

Once on a time, when a Halloween night came on the dark o' the moon, a lot o' old conjure wives was a-sittin' by the fire an' a-cookin' a big supper for theirselves.

The wind was a-howlin' 'round like it does on Halloween nights, an' the old conjure wives they hitched theirselves up to the fire an' talked about the spells they was a-goin' to weave long come midnight.

By an' by there come a knockin' at the door.

"Who's there?" called an old conjure wife. "Who-o? Who-o?"

"One who is hungry and cold," said a voice.

Then the old conjure wives, they all burst out laughin' an' they called out:

> "We's a-cookin' for ourselves.
> Who'll cook for you?
> Who? Who?"

The voice didn't say nothin', but the knockin' just kept on.

122

"Who's that a-knockin'?" called out another conjure wife. "Who? Who?"

Then there come a whistlin', wailin' sound:

> "Let me in, do-o-o-o!
> I'se cold thro-o-o-o an' thro-o-o-o,
> An' I'se hungry too-o-o!"

Then the old conjure wives, they all burst out laughin', an' they commenced to sing out:

> "Git along, do!
> We's a-cookin' for ourselves.
> Who'll cook for you?
> Who? Who?"

The voice didn't say nothin', but the knockin' just kept on.

Then the old conjure wives they went to work a-cookin' of the supper for theirselves, an' the voice didn't say nothin', but the knockin' just kept on.

An' then the old conjure wives they hitched up to the fire an' they ate an' ate—an' the voice didn't say nothin', but the knockin' just kept on. An' the old conjure wives they called out again:

> "Go 'way, do!
> We's a-cookin' for ourselves.
> Who'll cook for you?
> Who? Who?"

An' the voice didn't say nothin', but the knockin' just kept on.

Then the old conjure wives began to get scared-like, an' one of 'em says, "Let's give it somethin' an' get it away before it spoils our spells."

An' the voice didn't say nothin', but the knockin' just kept on.

Then the old conjure wives they took the littlest piece of dough, as big as a pea, an' they put it in the fry pan.

123

An' the voice didn't say nothin', but the knockin' just kept on.

An' when they put the dough in the fry pan it begun to swell an' swell, an' it swelled over the fry pan an' it swelled over the top o' the stove an' it swelled out on the floor.

An' the voice didn't say nothin', but the knockin' just kept on.

Then the old conjure wives got scared an' they ran for the door, an' the *door was shut tight*.

An' the voice didn't say nothin', but the knockin' just kept on.

An' then the dough it swelled an' it swelled all over the floor an' it swelled up into the chairs. An' the old conjure wives they climbed up on the backs of the chairs an' they were scareder and scareder. An' they called out, "Who's that a-knockin' at the door? Who? Who?"

An' the voice didn't say nothin', but the knockin' just kept on.

An' the dough kept a-swellin' an' a-swellin', an' the old conjure wives begun to scrooge up smaller an' smaller, an' their eyes got bigger an' bigger with scaredness, an' they kept a-callin', "Who's that a-knockin'? Who? Who?"

An' then the knockin' stopped, and the voice called out,

> *"Fly out the window, do!*
> *There's no more house for you!"*

An' the old conjure wives they spread their wings an' they flew out the windows an' off into the woods, all a-callin', "Who'll cook for you? Who? Who?"

An' now if you go into the woods in the dark o' the moon you'll see the old conjure wife owls an' hear 'em callin', "Who'll cook for you? Who-o! Who-o!"

Only on a Halloween night you don't want to go 'round the old owls, because *then* they turns to old conjure wives a-weavin' their spells.

Wiley and the Hairy Man

Wiley's pappy was a bad man and no-count. He stole watermelons in the dark of the moon. He was lazy, too, and slept while the weeds grew higher than the cotton. Worse still, he killed three martins and never even chunked at a crow.

One day he fell off the ferry boat where the river is quicker than anywhere else and no one ever found him. They looked for him a long way down river and in the still pools between the sand-banks, but they never found him. They heard a big man laughing across the river, and everybody said, "That's the Hairy Man." So they stopped looking.

"Wiley," his mammy told him, "the Hairy Man's got your pappy and he's goin' to get you if you don't look out."

"Yas'm," he said. "I'll look out. I'll take my hound-dogs everywhere I go. The Hairy Man can't stand no hound-dog."

Wiley knew that because his mammy had told him. She knew because she came from the swamps by the Tombisbee River and knew conjure magic.

One day Wiley took his axe and went down in the

swamp to cut some poles for a hen-roost and his hounds went with him. But they took out after a shoat* and ran it so far off Wiley couldn't even hear them yelp.

"Well," he said, "I hope the Hairy Man ain't nowhere round here now."

He picked up his axe to start cutting poles, but he looked up and there came the Hairy Man through the trees grinning. He was sure ugly and his grin didn't help much. He was hairy all over. His eyes burned like fire and spit drooled all over his big teeth.

"Don't look at me like that," said Wiley, but the Hairy Man kept coming and grinning, so Wiley threw down his axe and climbed up a big bay tree. He saw the Hairy Man didn't have feet like a man but like a cow, and Wiley never had seen a cow up a bay tree.

"What for you done climb up there?" the Hairy Man asked Wiley when he got to the bottom of the tree.

Wiley climbed nearly to the top of the tree and looked down. Then he climbed plumb to the top.

"How come you climbin' trees?" the Hairy Man said.

"My mammy done tole me to stay away from you. What you got in that big croaker-sack †?"

"I ain't got nothin' yet."

"Gwan away from here," said Wiley, hoping the tree would grow some more.

"Ha," said the Hairy Man and picked up Wiley's axe. He swung it about and the chips flew. Wiley grabbed the tree close, rubbed his belly on it and hollered, "Fly, chips, fly, back in your same old place."

The chips flew and the Hairy Man cussed and damned. Then he swung the axe and Wiley knew he'd have to holler fast. They went to it tooth and toe-nail then, Wiley hollering and the Hairy Man chopping. He hollered till he was hoarse and he saw the Hairy Man was gaining on him.

*young pig
†a sack for gathering frogs.

127

"I'll come down part of the way," he said, "if you'll make this bay tree twice as big around."

"I ain't studyin' you," said the Hairy Man, swinging the axe.

"I bet you can't," said Wiley.

"I ain't going to try," said the Hairy Man.

Then they went to it again, Wiley hollering and the Hairy Man chopping. Wiley had about yelled himself out when he heard his hound-dogs yelping way off.

"Hyeaaah, dog," hollered Wiley, and they both heard the hound-dogs yelping and coming jam-up. The Hairy Man looked worried.

"Come on down," he said, "and I'll teach you conjure."

"I can learn all the conjure I want from my mammy."

The Hairy Man cussed some more, but he threw the axe down and took off through the swamp.

When Wiley got home he told his mammy that the Hairy Man had most got him, but his dogs ran him off.

"Did he have his sack?"

"Yas'm."

"Next time he come after you, don't you climb no bay tree."

"I ain't," said Wiley. "They ain't big enough around."

"Don't climb no kind o' tree. Just stay on the ground and say 'Hello, Hairy Man.' You hear me, Wiley?"

"No'm."

"He ain't goin' to hurt you, child. You can put the Hairy Man in the dirt when I tell you how to do him."

"I puts him in the dirt and he puts me in that croaker-sack. I ain't puttin' no Hairy Man in the dirt."

"You just do like I say. You say, 'Hello, Hairy Man.' He says, 'Hello, Wiley,' You say, 'Hairy Man, I done heard you about the best conjureman 'round here.' 'I reckon I am.' You say, 'I bet you cain't turn yourself into no giraffe.' You keep tellin' him he cain't and he will. Then you say, 'I bet you cain't turn yourself into no 'possum.' Then he will, and you grab him and throw him in the sack."

129

"It don't sound just right somehow," said Wiley, "but I will." So he tied up his dogs so they wouldn't scare away the Hairy Man, and went down to the swamp again. He hadn't been there long when he looked up and there came the Hairy Man grinning through the trees, hairy all over and his big teeth showing more than ever. He knew Wiley came off without his hound-dogs. Wiley nearly climbed a tree when he saw the croaker-sack, but he didn't.

"Hello, Hairy Man," he said.

"Hello, Wiley." He took the sack off his shoulder and started opening it up.

"Hairy Man, I done heard you are about the best conjure man round here."

"I reckon I is."

"I bet you cain't turn yourself into no giraffe."

"Shucks, that ain't no trouble," said the Hairy Man.

"I bet you cain't do it."

So the Hairy Man twisted round and turned himself into a giraffe.

"I bet you cain't turn yourself into no alligator," said Wiley.

The giraffe twisted around and turned into an alligator, all the time watching Wiley to see he didn't try to run.

"Anybody can turn theyself into something big as a man," said Wiley, "but I bet you cain't turn yourself into no 'possum."

The alligator twisted around and turned into a 'possum, and Wiley grabbed it and threw it in the sack.

Wiley tied the sack up as tight as he could and then he threw it in the river. He started home through the swamp and he looked up and there came the Hairy Man grinning through the trees. Wiley had to scramble up the nearest tree.

The Hairy Man gloated: "I turned myself into the wind and blew out. Wiley, I'm going to set right here till you get hungry and fall out of that bay tree. You want me to learn you some more conjure?"

Wiley studied a while. He studied about the Hairy Man

and he studied about his hound-dogs tied up most a mile away.

"Well," he said, "you done some pretty smart tricks. But I bet you cain't make things disappear and go where nobody knows."

"Huh, that's what I'm good at. Look at that old bird-nest on the limb. Now look. It's done gone."

"How I know it was there in the first place? I bet you cain't make something I know is there disappear."

"Ha ha!" said the Hairy Man. "Look at your shirt."

Wiley looked down and his shirt was gone, but he didn't care, because that was just what he wanted the Hairy Man to do.

"That was just a plain old shirt," he said. "But this rope I got tied round my breeches has been conjured. I bet you cain't make it disappear."

"Huh, I can make all the rope in this county disappear."

"Ha ha ha," said Wiley.

The Hairy Man looked mad and threw his chest way out. He opened his mouth wide and hollered loud.

"From now on all the rope in this county has done disappeared."

Wiley reared back, holding his breeches with one hand and a tree-limb with the other.

"Hyeaaah, dog," he hollered loud enough to be heard more than a mile off.

When Wiley and his dogs got back home his mammy asked him did he put the Hairy Man in the sack.

"Yes'm, but he done turned himself into the wind and blew right through that old croaker-sack."

"That is bad," said his mammy. "But you done fool him twice. If you fool him again he'll leave you alone. He'll be mighty hard to fool the third time."

"We got to study up a way to fool him, mammy."

"I'll study up a way tereckly," she said, and sat down by the fire and held her chin between her hands and studied real hard. But Wiley wasn't studying anything

131

except how to keep the Hairy Man away. He took his hound-dogs out and tied one at the back door and one at the front door. Then he crossed a broom and an axe-handle over the window and built a fire in the fire-place. Feeling a lot safer, he sat down and helped his mammy study. After a little while his mammy said, "Wiley, you go down to the pen and get that little suckin' pig away from that old sow."

Wiley went down and snatched the sucking pig through the rails and left the sow grunting and heaving in the pen. He took the pig back to his mammy and she put it in his bed.

"Now, Wiley," she said, "you go on up to the loft and hide."

So he did. Before long he heard the wind howling and the trees shaking, and then his dogs started growling. He looked out through a knot-hole in the planks and saw the dog at the front door looking down toward the swamps, with his hair standing up and his lips drawn back in a snarl. Then an animal as big as a mule with horns on its head ran out of the swamp past the house. The dog jerked and jumped, but he couldn't get loose. Then an animal bigger than a great big dog with a long nose and big teeth ran out of the swamp and growled at the cabin. This time the dog broke loose and took after the big animal, who ran back down into the swamp. Wiley looked out another chink at the back end of the loft just in time to see his other dog jerk loose and take out after an animal which might have been a 'possum, but wasn't.

"Law-dee," said Wiley. "The Hairy Man is coming here, sure."

He didn't have long to wait, because soon enough he heard something with feet like a cow scrambling around on the roof. He knew it was the Hairy Man, because he heard him swear when he touched the hot chimney. The Hairy Man jumped off the roof when he found out there was a fire in the fire-place and came up and knocked on the front door as big as you please.

"Mammy," he hollered, "I done come after your baby."

"You ain't going to get him," mammy hollered back.

"Give him here or I'll set your house on fire with light-ning."

"I got plenty of sweet-milk to put it out with."

"Give him here or I'll dry up your spring, make your cow go dry and send a million boll-weevils out of the ground to eat up your cotton."

"Hairy Man, you wouldn't do all that. That's mighty mean."

"I'm a mighty mean man. I ain't never seen a man as mean as I am."

"If I give you my baby will you go on way from here and leave everything else alone?"

"I swear that's just what I'll do," said the Hairy Man, so mammy opened the door and let him in.

"He's over there in that bed," she said.

The Hairy Man came in grinning like he was meaner than he said. He walked over to the bed and snatched the covers back.

"Hey," he hollered, "there ain't nothing in this bed but a old suckin' pig."

"I ain't said what kind of baby I was giving you, and that suckin' pig sure belong to me before I gave it to you."

The Hairy Man raged and yelled. He stomped all over the house gnashing his teeth. Then he grabbed up the pig and tore out through the swamp, knocking down trees right and left. The next morning the swamp had a wide path like a cyclone had cut through it, with trees torn loose at the roots and lying on the ground. When the Hairy Man was gone Wiley came down from the loft.

"Is he done gone, mammy?"

"Yes, child. That old Hairy Man cain't ever hurt you again. We done fool him three times."

Jean Sotte

There was once a fellow who was so foolish that everybody called him Jean Sotte. He was so simple that every one made fun of him. He would light the lamp in daytime, and put it out at night; he would take an umbrella with him only when it was very dark. In summer he would put on a great coat, and in winter he would go nearly naked. In short, he did everything contrary to common sense. King Bangon, who loved to play tricks, heard of the sayings and deeds of Jean Sotte, and sent for him to amuse his friends. When Jean came to the king all began to laugh, as he looked so awkward. The king asked him if he knew how to count. Jean replied that he knew how to count eggs; that yesterday he had found four and two. "How many does that make?" said the king. Jean went to count the eggs, and on returning said there were four and two.

"Exactly," said the king, "but tell me, Jean Sotte, they say that Compair Lapin* is your father?"

"Yes, he is."

* Brer Rabbit.

"No, no," said some one else; "I think it is Compair Bouki."

"Yes, yes," said Jean Sotte; "it is he also."

"No, no," said an old woman who was passing; "it is Renard* who is your father."

"Yes," said Jean Sotte, "all of them; they are all my fathers. Every time one of them passes by me he says, 'Good-morning, my child.' I must believe, then, that they are all my fathers."

Everybody laughed at Jean Sotte; then the king said: "Jean Sotte, I want you to bring me to-morrow morning a bottle of bull's milk. It is to make a drug for my daughter, who is sick, and has a sideache in her back."

"All right," said Jean Sotte, "to-morrow morning early I shall bring it."

King Bangon then said:—

"On the first of April, in one month, you will come. I want you to guess something. If you guess, I will give you my daughter in marriage, but if you try three times, and do not succeed, my executioner will have to cut your neck."

"All right," said Jean Sotte, "I will try." And then he went away, pretending to go and get the bull's milk.

When he reached home, he related to his mother all that had happened, and the old woman began to cry, and could not be consoled, because, however foolish her boy was, she loved him, as he was her only child. She forbade him to go to the king, and threatened to tie him in her cabin, or to have the sheriff throw him in prison. Jean Sotte paid no attention to his mother, and started before daybreak, with his axe on his shoulder. He soon arrived at the house of the king, and he climbed into a big oak-tree which was before the door. He began, "caou, caou, caou," to cut down the branches with his axe, and he woke up everybody in the house. One of the servants of the king came out to see what was the matter; and when he saw Jean Sotte on the top of

* Fox.

the tree, he said: "But what is your business there? Fool that you are, you are disturbing everybody."

"It is not your business,—do you hear?" said Jean Sotte. "Are you the watch-dog to be barking thus in the yard? When your master, King Bangon, comes, I will tell him what I am doing here."

The king came out, and asked Jean Sotte what he was doing there. He replied that he was cutting the bark to make some tea for his father, who had been delivered the day before of two twins.

"What!" said the king, "for whom do you take me, Jean Sotte. Where did you ever hear of a man in childbirth? I think you mean to make fun of me."

"How is it that yesterday you asked for a bottle of bull's milk. If you were right, I am also."

The king replied: "I believe that you are not so foolish as you want to make people believe. Go to the kitchen, and they will give you your breakfast. Don't forget to come on the first of April, that we may see which of us will be the April fool."

On the first of April Jean Sotte mounted his horse and went out without his mother seeing him. Compair Bouki, who is deceitful and evil-minded, said: "I shall prevent Jean Sotte from going, because I know he is so foolish that they will cut his neck and keep his horse. It is better that I should profit by it, and take his horse. Don't you say anything; you will see what I shall do."

He took a large basket full of poisoned cakes, and put it on a bridge where Jean Sotte was to pass. "If he eats those cakes, he will die, and I shall take the horse."

Bouki knew that Jean Sotte was greedy and that he would surely eat the cakes. Compair Lapin liked Jean Sotte, because one day, when he was caught in a snare, Jean Sotte had freed him. He did not forget that, and said: "I want to protect the poor fellow," and before daybreak he waited on the road for Jean Sotte. When he saw him, he said: "Jean Sotte, I am coming to render you a service, listen to me: don't eat or drink anything on your way, even if you are dying of hunger and of thirst; and when the king will ask you to guess, you will reply what I am going to tell you. Come near: I don't want anybody to hear."

Compair Lapin then told him what to say. "Yes, yes, I understand," said Jean Sotte, and he began to laugh.

"Now," said Compair Lapin, "don't forget me when you marry the king's daughter; we can have good business together."

"Yes," said Jean Sotte, "I shall not forget you."

"Well, good luck, pay attention to all you see, look on all sides, and listen well."

Then Jean Sotte started, and a little while afterwards he arrived at a bridge on the river. The first thing he saw was the basket full of cakes which Compair Bouki had placed there. They smelled good and they were very tempting. Jean Sotte touched them and felt like biting one, but he remembered what Compair Lapin had told him. He stopped a moment and said: "Let me see if they will do harm to my horse." He took half a dozen cakes and gave them to his horse. The poor beast died almost immediately and fell on the bridge. "See, if I had not been prudent, it is I who would be dead instead of my horse. Ah! Compair Lapin was right; a little more and I should have been lost. Now I shall have to go on foot."

Before he started he threw his horse into the river; and as the poor beast was being carried away by the current, three buzzards alighted on the horse and began to eat him. Jean Sotte looked at him a long time, until he disappeared behind the point in the river. "Compair Lapin told me: 'Listen, look, and don't say anything;' all right, I shall have something to ask the king to guess."

When Jean Sotte came to the king nobody was trying to guess, for all those who had tried three times had been put to death by the king's executioner. Fifty men already had been killed, and every one said, on seeing Jean Sotte: "There is Jean Sotte who is going to try, they will surely cut off his head, for he is so foolish. But so much the worse for him if he is such a fool."

When he saw Jean Sotte the king began to laugh and told him to come nearer. "What is it," said he, "that early in the morning walks on four legs, at noon on two, and in the evening on three legs?"

"If I guess, you will give me your daughter?"

"Yes," said the king.

"Oh! that is nothing to guess."

"Well, hurrah! Hurry on if you don't want me to cut your neck."

Jean Sotte told him, it was a child who walked on four legs; when he grew up he walked on two, and when he grew old he had to take a stick, and that made three legs.

All remained with their mouths wide open, they were so astonished.

"You have guessed right; my daughter is for you. Now, let anybody ask me something, as I know everything in the world; if I do not guess right I will give him my kingdom and my fortune."

Jean Sotte said to the king: "I saw a dead being that was carrying three living beings and was nourishing them. The dead did not touch the land and was not in the sky; tell me what it is, or I shall take your kingdom and your fortune."

King Bangon tried to guess; he said that and that and a thousand things, but he had to give it up. Jean Sotte said then: "My horse died on a bridge, I threw him into the river, and three buzzards alighted on him and were eating him up in the river. They did not touch the land and they were not in the sky."

Everybody saw that Jean Sotte was smarter than all of them together. He married the king's daughter, took his place, and governed the kingdom. He took Compair Lapin as his first overseer, and hanged Compair Bouki for his rascality. After that they changed Jean Sotte's name and called him Jean l'Esprit.

*European Tales Brought by
Immigrants*

How Jack Went to Seek his Fortune

Once upon a time there was a boy named Jack, and one morning he started to go and seek his fortune.

He hadn't gone very far before he met a cat.

"Where are you going, Jack?" said the cat.

"I am going to seek my fortune."

"May I go with you?"

"Yes," said Jack, "the more the merrier."

So on they went, jiggelty-jolt, jiggelty-jolt.

They went a little further and they met a dog.

"Where are you going, Jack?" said the dog.

"I am going to seek my fortune."

"May I go with you?"

"Yes," said Jack, "the more the merrier."

So on they went, jiggelty-jolt, jiggelty-jolt.

They went on a little further and they met a goat.

"Where are you going, Jack?" said the goat.

"I am going to seek my fortune."

"May I go with you?"

"Yes," said Jack, "the more the merrier."

So on they went, jiggelty-jolt, jiggelty-jolt.

They went a little further and they met a bull.

"Where are you going, Jack?" said the bull.
"I am going to seek my fortune."
"May I go with you?"
"Yes," said Jack, "the more the merrier."
So on they went, jiggelty-jolt, jiggelty-jolt.
They went a little further and they met a skunk.
"Where are you going, Jack?" said the skunk.
"I am going to seek my fortune."
"May I go with you?"
"Yes," said Jack, "the more the merrier."
So on they went, jiggelty-jolt, jiggelty-jolt.
They went a little further and they met a rooster.
"Where are you going, Jack?" said the rooster.
"I am going to seek my fortune."
"May I go with you?"
"Yes," said Jack, "the more the merrier."
So on they went, jiggelty-jolt, jiggelty-jolt.
 Well, they went on till it was about dark, and they began

to think of some place where they could spend the night. About this time they came in sight of a house, and Jack told them to keep still while he went up and looked in through the window. And there were some robbers counting over their money. Then Jack went back and told them to wait till he gave the word, and then to make all the noise they could. So when they were all ready Jack gave the word, and the cat mewed, the dog barked, and the goat blatted, and the bull bellowed, and the rooster crowed, and all together they made such a dreadful noise that it frightened the robbers all away.

And then they went in and took possession of the house. Jack was afraid the robbers would come back in the night, and so when it came time to go to bed he put the cat in the rocking-chair, and he put the dog under the table, and he put the goat up-stairs, and he put the bull down cellar, and he put the skunk in the corner of the fireplace, and the rooster flew up on to the roof, and Jack went to bed.

By and by the robbers saw it was all dark and they sent one man back to the house to look after their money. Before long he came back in a great fright and told them his story.

"I went back to the house," said he, "and went in and tried to sit down in the rocking-chair, and there was an old woman knitting, and she stuck her knitting-needles into me.

"I went to the table to look after the money and there was a shoemaker under the table, and he stuck his awl into me.

"I started to go up-stairs, and there was a man up there threshing, and he knocked me down with his flail.

"I started to go down cellar, and there was a man down there chopping wood, and he knocked me up with his axe.

"I went to warm me at the fireplace, and there was an old woman washing dishes, and she threw her dish-water on to me.

"But I shouldn't have minded all that if it hadn't been for that little fellow on top of the house, who kept a-hollering 'Toss him up to me-e!' Toss him up to me-e!'"

Twist-mouth Family

Once there was a family of people who lived in the back country far off from any town. The whole family had very funny mouths.

The father's lower lip and lower jaw stuck way, way out.

The mother's upper lip was incredibly long and hung down over the lower.

The oldest girl's mouth was twisted to the right, so that she had to talk, eat, and sing out of the right side of her mouth.

The brother's mouth was twisted to the left, so that he had to eat, talk, and laugh out of the left side of his mouth.

The youngest boy had a mouth just like anyone, but in this family that too was different.

When the children grew up, and it came time for them to go to college, the two oldest said No, they'd rather stay at home with their own kin than have to go out in the world with all those straight-faced people.

But the youngest boy said Yes, he'd like to go to college. So he went.

Time went by and then the youngest boy came home for Christmas vacation.

Everybody looked forward to seeing him and hearing the news of the world. And the mother baked a big cake to celebrate.

That night the family sat around the table eating cake and listening to the adventures of the youngest brother who had been so far from home.

The cake was very good.

The father had to hold his piece way up and push it down into his mouth.

The mother had to shove her piece up under her upper lip to get it into her mouth.

The oldest girl ate daintily, poking one small piece after another into the right side of her mouth.

The brother jammed big hunks into the left side of his.

The youngest brother ate just like anyone.

It grew late and the time came to go to bed.

"Father, will you blow out the light?" said the mother.

"Yes, I will."

"Well, do," said the mother.

"Well, I will," said the father.

So the man leaned over the lamp and blew. But his under lip was so big that he could only blow up—this way—and he could not blow out the light.

"Mother, you do it," said the man.

"All right, I will."

"Well, do."

"Well, I will."

So the woman blew and blew. She blew this way—and could not blow out the lamp.

"Daughter, you do it," said the mother.

"All right, I will."

"Well, do."

"Well, I will."

So the daughter tried to blow the light out. She blew this way—and could not blow out the light.

"Here—you do it," said the girl to the brother.

"All right," said the boy, "I'll do it."

145

"Well, do."

"Well, I will."

So the brother tried. He blew this way—and could not blow out the light.

"You do it," said the brother to the youngest boy.

"Sure!" said the youngest boy.

"Wh——ff" he went (like that), and the light was out.

Everybody was delighted. Now they could all go to bed.

"Wonderful thing—a college education," said the father.

A Stepchild that Was Treated
Mighty Bad

Hearing some women talking about a man over at Vest marrying again and pondering with them on how his new woman will treat her stepchild, his pretty little girl, put me in mind of an olden tale about a stepchild that was treated mighty bad. Set down and rest yourself a little minute while I tell.

They was a man and a woman, not nobody you ever heard tell of, but way back in time. Everybody has done forgot their names. A king and a queen they are said to have been, anyhow that's what I always heard tell. They had an onliest child, a girl it was, and pretty as a picture; good too, I reckon. Named her Snow White and Rose Red on account of her skin was white as snow in wintertime and her cheeks were red like blooms on the rosebushes in the summertime.

The way some folks tell the tale, the mother died when she birthed little Snow White. Some tells that she had a fever. I don't know; anyhow, she died and left her man and the baby. On her deathbed she made her man promise not to marry again and bring no stepmother to be mean to

Snow White. He made promise, and I don't misdoubt he aimed at the time to do like he promised. But he had to hire somebody to do the needful things for his child that it takes a woman to do anyways right.

Well, the nurse-woman was a clever person, not bad-looking, neither. She made little Snow White like her and acted real motherly and nice. The man took notice how good she tended Snow White. Then he started to notice she weren't bad-looking. First thing you know, he was a-courting her—just what she had in her mind from the first minute she hired herself out to take care of Snow White for him. Pretty soon he named marrying, the promise he made to his dead wife gone clean out of his mind. The nurse-woman jumped at the chance, and so they got married and she moved her house plunder to his house and rented out her place for cash money.

When Snow White got to be of an age to be noticed for being pretty in a way to make womenfolk jealous of her, her stepmother turned poison mean. She wanted to be the best-looking woman in the neighborhood, and she treated pretty girls like poison, more especially her stepchild that was far and away the prettiest girl that ever lived in the neighborhood.

The stepmother had a looking glass hung up on her wall and she loved to look at herself in it and think how pretty. It made her so mad to see how her stepchild was better favored in looks than she was her ownself that she couldn't hardly stand it. She would stand there and sass her looking glass for not making her look pretty all the time. Some tells how the looking glass sassed her back and always told her Snow White was far and away the prettiest. I don't never tell it that-a-way, for I ain't got no faith in a looking glass that talks.

This mean-hearted woman thought up ways to get rid of Snow White. She said one day to a strange man going by with a gun and a hound-dog like he was going to hunt in the wood, "I'll give you six bits, maybe a dollar, if you will toll this girl off in the woods a far piece and leave her there to perish. I purely can't stand the sight of her any longer." He wouldn't promise till she gave him ten dollars and six bits, all the cash money she had. Then he tolled the girl off, telling her he could show her fine places to pick flower blooms in the woods.

Once he got her way back in the deep woods, a far piece from home, he slipped off and left her picking wild flower blooms. But his hound-dog stayed with her, close by to be a protection. So the man had ten dollars and six bits in his pockets for doing a mean-hearted thing; but he lost a good hunting dog, though I don't know how much it woulda been worth.

Come night, the hound-dog led her to a little house he had found and it had beds and things in it. The dog went off somewhere, and Snow White flew busy and cooked up a good supper. She waited for somebody to come and eat up what she cooked; but, when they never came, she had much as she wanted for supper and put the rest of the supper in the cupboard in the cook room.

Seven rocking chairs she found in the house, and she rocked as much as she wanted to till she felt rested. Then she found seven beds, all made up smooth and nice but one. It was all rumpled up, and she smoothed out the covers and fixed it nice. Then she laid down and went to sleep.

Seven little men came home from the day's work chopping trees in the woods. Rummaging in the cupboard, they found what Snow White cooked; and they washed their hands and had a good supper. They rocked a while to rest from the hard day's work, and then they got sleepy. They went upstairs to the room with their beds all in a row, and they found Snow White. They tipped around, being quiet, and didn't wake her up at all. One of the little men slept on a pallet bed on the floor so Snow White could sleep on his good soft bed.

Come morning, they made their manners to Snow White, and they asked her to be a sister to them and keep their house tidy and cook and sew, and they would make her a good living, and they would dearly love to have her for their sister. The hound-dog came back and stayed with her in the daytime to be a protection while the little men chopped in the woods. Of nights the dog would go off somewheres.

After a time the mean-hearted stepmother found out that Snow White was still living and getting prettier every day of her life. So the stepmother fixed herself up so Snow White wouldn't know her and went to the little house in the woods where Snow White lived with the little men. And the hound-dog barked and raised his bristles, but she looked like an old woman peddling things around the country. And Snow White made the hound-dog hush up and lay down.

The stepmother had a golden comb that she gave to Snow White. When she put it in Snow White's hair, she fell down like dead for the comb had poison in it. Then the old woman went off.

The dog went and fetched the little men to come see about Snow White. They pulled the poison comb out of her hair and she got right up and cooked supper. They told her not to let no strangers come in the house when they went off to their job of work.

Another time the mean-hearted stepmother found out Snow White had come alive. She had to think up a new way to get shut of her. She put some poison on a finger ring and sent it to Snow White. I don't know how, maybe by a neighbor passing through. Anyhow, the finger ring made Snow White fall down like dead. The hound-dog went and fetched the little men from their job of work, and they pulled off the finger ring, and Snow White got up and cooked supper.

The last time it was some fine apples the mean-hearted stepmother sent to Snow White. The finest red apple had

151

poison in it, and Snow White had scarce swallowed ary bite till she fell down dead with a piece of apple in her mouth. That time the hound went and fetched the little men, but they didn't see nothing to pull off of her to make her come to. So they had to give her up for dead. They laid her out in a coffin with glass so they could look at her. They fixed flower blossoms fresh around the coffin every day after they put it in a church up a mountain. The hound-dog stayed by it to guard it from harm.

One day a fine man, maybe a king, came along and looked through the glass coffin at Snow White. The hound-dog liked the man and let him look. The man loved Snow White and wanted to have her with him. When the little men came home from work, he talked and coaxed till they let him carry Snow White in her glass coffin home with him to his big fine house. Going down the mountain, he dropped the coffin, though he didn't aim to. Being dropped jarred the piece of apple out of Snow White's mouth and she came alive again. They went back to the little house and told the little men about it, and they let Snow White marry him and go and live in his big fine house.

At his house she didn't have to cook and keep house, so she took the hound-dog for protection and went a-walking about the place. Some old apple trees were all bowed down and about to break. They begged her to shake their limbs and make some of the apples fall off so they wouldn't break. And she was glad to do it. Then some cows asked her would she milk out their bags so they wouldn't get all sore. And she was glad to do it. Then she came to an old woman with a heavy basket. And she was more than glad to carry the old woman's basket, not even waiting to get asked. I reckon the old woman went home with her and stayed all night. Anyhow, in the morning the old woman said to her, "You can keep that old basket to pay back for your trouble."

When the old woman had gone off, Snow White opened

up the lid of the basket and it was full of all kinds of fine clothes made of gold and jewels besides a heap of other pretties more than just clothes to wear.

Snow White dressed up fine and her man thought she was mighty pretty. Then they went to visit her daddy, and they took the old woman's basket full of things, for the more Snow White took fine things out, the more the basket got full of things again. And she filled her daddy's pockets up full of gold money and made him a present of some more golden things. And she even made a present to her mean-hearted stepmother.

And the mean-hearted stepmother tried to steal the basket away from Snow White. But when she took hold of it, the basket got so heavy she couldn't lift it or even budge it one bit, and she couldn't take nothing out of it neither.

So after Snow White went back home, with her man a-carrying her fine basket, the mean-hearted stepmother took it in her head to do just like Snow White and get her a fine basket of golden money and things to wear and jewels and other pretties.

She walked through the woods to the house where the seven little men lived. They were off at work, but she never turned her hand to do a thing about the place. She just sat down and rocked all day till she broke down all the rocking chairs and left the pieces piled up in a heap. Then she laid down to sleep and rumpled up all the beds. The little men ran her off and wouldn't put up with her at all.

She walked around in the woods hunting a place to stay all night, and I don't know if she found any place or how she made out. I reckon I just forgot that part.

Anyhow, come morning, she met up with the apple trees that had too many apples again, for what Snow White left on the trees had got bigger and heavier. The orchard trees asked the mean-hearted stepmother would she shake their limbs and make some of the apples fall off so they wouldn't break and she said she never aimed to do no hard work, and she walked on.

The cows asked her would she milk out their bags so they wouldn't get all sore. But she wouldn't do that neither.

She kept on walking and looking for the old woman with the basket full of fine things. After a time, she found the old woman setting down to rest. The mean-hearted old step-mother never even said, "Howdy." She grabbed up the basket and ran off fast as she could. Whenever she got home, she opened up the basket quick as she could and made a grab. She nearly fell down dead in a fright when she saw what she grabbed—handful of snakes and toad-frogs. She flung them away in the weeds and tried to empty out the basket. But it stayed full to the brim with toad-frogs and snakes, full of poison and mean as could be.

When her man saw what she fetched home that he couldn't get rid of, he left her and went to live with Snow White and her man in his big fine house.

The mean-hearted stepmother got killed to be rid of her meanness but I don't know how she got killed. And it don't make me no difference.

Nippy and the Yankee Doodle

A yankee doodle is a pottery fife with five finger holes.

Once there was an old woman who had three sons named Jim, John and Nippy. One weekend Jim and John told their mother to bake them a cake because they's going to see their girls. Nippy, the youngest and the one they thought foolish, spoke up and said, "Let me go with you."

And they said, "No, you're a foolish boy and you had better stay home with your mammy."

They started out and Nippy went to his mother and said, "Mommy, bake me a cake. I want to go and foller my brothers."

And she says, "All right, Nippy, if you'll take the riddle and go down to the spring and get me a riddle full of water I'll bake you a cake." She thought this would be a way to keep him at home.

He went down to the spring with the riddle, dipped it up full of water and started. It all poured out of course right on through it. He'd dip it up again and it'd pour out. He tried it several times and never got started with no water. And he heard a little bird up on a tree, said,

Daub it with moss and slick it with clay
And you can carry your water away.

He looked up and said, "What did you say, little bird?"
It said,

Daub it with moss and slick it with clay
And you can carry your water away.

So he daubed the riddle with moss and then slicked it
over good with clay, filled it up with water and went to the
house. His mother thought he had done a smart trick so
she baked him a big cake and put it in a poke and let him set
out follering his brothers. Caught up with 'em sometimes
that evening, and that night they went to see an old man's
three daughters that lived by the river.

Next morning the oldest boy Jim wanted to marry the
man's oldest daughter, and the old man says, "I'll tell ye
what I'll do," says, "you go over to that old man's house
across the river and get his three gold lockets and gold
staff," and says, "I'll let you marry my oldest daughter."

So all three of them went across the river where the old
man lived and asked to stay all night. He let 'em come in
and stay. He had three daughters and they all slept on
pallets on the floor, the girls on one side and the boys on
the other. Nippy he was kinda scared and stayed awake
till a long way in the night. Some time before the fire went
out the old man come in and he brought three gold lockets
and put around his three girls' necks and then eased out of
the room. So Nippy saw what he was doing and was afraid
he would come back in and kill the ones that didn't have
gold lockets on. When everything got quiet again he eased
over and took the gold lockets off the girls' necks and put
'em on him and his brothers' necks.

Some time later in the night the old man come in and cut
his three daughters' throats. Next morning right at the
edge of daylight, why, Nippy got his brothers up and they
took the three lockets and the old man's gold staff and
headed back across the river. About the time they got
across the river the old man come to the edge of the river
and called, "Hey, Nippy, when are you comin' back?"

Said, "You've caused me to kill my three girls and you've stole my three gold lockets and my gold staff," Said, "When are you comin' back to see me?"

Said, "I'll be back some time, Grandpa."

They went on in to the man's house and Jim married the man's oldest daughter. Some time the next day John wanted to marry the next oldest daughter, and the man says, "I'll tell you what I'll do," says, "if you'll go over the river to the old man's and get his halfmoon," says, "I'll give you two yoke of oxen, a half a bushel of gold and my daughter."

The next day the older boys talked around about how foolhardy Nippy was and got him to go over by himself. He went over there to get the halfmoon. The old man weren't at home but his old woman was making hominy.* He had to wait around awhile till she got the halfmoon to go in the dark kitchen to look at her hominy. She took a long time going to look at it, so Nippy eased up on the roof and started pouring salt down in the fire. The fire started crackling and burning blue blazes. The old man come in about that time, smelling around and said, "Old woman, you're burnin' your hominy up." She grabbed the halfmoon and run to look at her hominy, and Nippy pushed her on in the fire, grabbed the halfmoon and headed back across the river with it.

Time he got across the river the old man run to the edge and hollered at him, says, "Hey, Nippy," says, "when are you comin' back to see me?" and, "You caused me to kill my three girls, you stold my three lockets and stold my gold staff, and now you've pushed my old woman in the fire and gone with my halfmoon," says, "when are you comin' back?"

He said, "I'll be back to see you again, Grandpa."

He took the halfmoon in and give it to the old man. John got the two yoke of oxen, the half bushel of gold and the next oldest daughter.

*Maize, with the hulls removed from the kernels.

After the celebration Nippy decided he wanted to marry the youngest daughter and so he asked the old man for her. The old man says, "Tell ye what I'll do," says, "I'll give you two yoke of oxen, a half bushel of gold and my youngest daughter if you'll go back over to that old man's house and get his Yankee Doodle."

So he went over after the Yankee Doodle that evening. They were gone to church and about the time he got it and started he saw them coming. So he hid under the bed with the Yankee Doodle. Along after dark when the old man and the old woman went to bed, he started playing on the Yankee Doodle under there. The old woman said, "Old man, you're getting awful good all at once," said, "you just get back from church and start playing the Yankee Doodle."

He said , "Why, old woman, I've not thought of that Yankee Doodle in forty year."

She said, "Well, Nippy must be around again."

So he reached under the bed and pulled Nippy out, says, "Now I've got you this time, Nippy."

Nippy says, "What are you goin' to do with me, Grandpa?"

He sayd, "I'm going to kill ye!"

Says, "I wouldn't do that if I was you, Grandpa." Says, "If I had you" says, "I'd put ye up in the loft and feed ye on eggs and butter till you go right fat and then kill ye and invite all the neighbors in for a feast."

He says, "Well that's just what I'll do with you, Nippy."

So he put him up in the loft and fed him on eggs and butter for about two weeks and decided he was fat enough to kill. He went up and says, "Well, you're fat enough to kill now, Nippy. I'm goin' to lay you on the coolin' board."

Nippy says, "You don't have to take time to kill me, Grandpa." Says, "I'm easy killed and Grandma can do that while you go and invite all the neighbors and tell her to pop me in the oven for a feast."

So Grandma puts on the clay oven to get it right real hot.

She kept going to look at the oven to see if it was hot enough. And Nippy waited till it got real hot and when she went the next time he slipped up behind her and pushed her in the oven and popped the lid on her. He grabbed the Yankee Doodle and took back out across the river.

The old man come along about that time with some hungry neighbors, saw what Nippy had done. Said, "Hey, Nippy," says, "When are you comin' back to see me?" Says, "You caused me to kill my three daughters, you stold my three gold lockets and my gold staff, you pushed my old woman in the fire and stold my Yankee Doodle." Says, "Now when are you comin' back to see me?"

Nippy says, "I don't guess I'll ever be back to see ye, Grandpa."

He took the Yankee Doodle back to the old man and got his two yoke of oxen, the half bushel of gold and the youngest daughter to marry. Nippy played the Yankee Doodle while they all danced and celebrated their weddings. They took their oxen and their gold and their wives home, built houses and settled down and lived happy ever after.

Old Fire Dragaman

One time Jack and his two brothers, Will and Tom, were all of 'em a-layin' around home; weren't none of 'em doin' no good so their daddy decided he'd set 'em to work. He had him a tract of land out in a wilderness of a place back up on the mountain. Told the boys they could go up there and work it. Said he'd give it to 'em. Hit was a right far ways from where anybody lived at, so they fixed 'em up a wagonload of rations and stuff for housekeepin' and pulled out.

There wasn't no house up there, so they cut poles and notched 'em up a shack. They had to go to work in a hurry to get out any crop and they set right in to clearin' 'em a newground. They decided one boy 'uld have to stay to the house till twelve and do the cookin'.

First day Tom and Jack left Will there. Will went to fixin' around and got dinner ready, went out and blowed the horn to call Tom and Jack, looked down the holler and there came a big old giant steppin' right up the mountain. Had him a pipe about four foot long, and he had a long old blue beard that dragged on the ground.

When Will saw the old giant was headed right for the

160

house, he ran and got behind the door, pulled it back on him and scrouged back against the wall a-shakin' like a leaf. The old giant came on to the house, reached in and throwed the cloth back off the dishes, eat ever'thing on the table in one bite and sopped the plates. Snatched him a chunk of fire and lit his pipe; the smoke came a-bilin' out. Then he wiped his mouth and went on back down the holler with that old pipe a-sendin' up smoke like a steam engine.

Tom and Jack came in directly, says, "Why in the world ain't ye got us no dinner, Will?"

"Law me!" says Will. "If you'd 'a seen what I just seen you'd 'a not thought about no dinner. An old Fire Draga-man came up here, eat ever' bite on the table, and sopped the plates."

Tom and Jack laughed right smart at Will.

Will says, "You all needn't to laugh. Hit'll be your turn tomorrow, Tom."

So they fixed up what vittles they could and they all went back to work in the newground.

Next day Tom got dinner, went out and blowed the horn. There came Old Fire Dragaman—

"Law me!" says Tom. "Where'll I get?"

He ran and scrambled under the bed. Old Fire Dragaman came on up, eat ever'thing there was on the table, sopped the plates, and licked out all the pots. Lit his old pipe and pulled out down the holler, the black smoke a-rollin' like comin' out a chimney. Hit was a sight to look at.

Will and Jack came in, says, "Where's our dinner, Tom?"

"Dinner, the nation! Old Fire Dragaman came back up here. Law me! Hit was the beatin'-est thing I ever seen!"

Will says, "Where was you at, Tom?"

"Well, I'll tell ye," says Tom; "I was down under the bed."

Jack laughed, and Will and Tom says, "You just wait about laughin', Jack. Hit'll be your time tomorrow."

Next day Will and Tom went to the newground. They

got to laughin' about where Jack 'uld hide at when Old Fire Dragaman came.

Jack fixed up ever'thing for dinner, went out about twelve and blowed the horn. Looked down the wilderness, there was Old Fire Dragaman a-comin' up the hill with his hands folded behind him and a-lookin' around this way and that.

Jack went on back in the house, started puttin' stuff on the table. Never paid no attention to the old giant, just went right on a-fixin' dinner. Old Fire Dragaman came on up.

Jack was scoopin' up a mess of beans out the pot, says, "Why, hello, Daddy."

"Howdy, son."

"Come on in, daddy. Get you a chair. Dinner's about ready; just stay and eat with us."

"No, I thank ye. I couldn't stay."

"Hits on the table. Come on sit down."

"No. I just stopped to light my pipe."

"Come on, daddy. Let's eat."

"No, much obliged. I got no time."

Old Fire Dragaman reached in to get him a coal of fire, got the biggest chunk in the fireplace, stuck it down in his old pipe, and started on back. Jack took out and follered him with all that smoke a-bilin' out; watched where he went to, and saw him go down a big straight hole in the ground.

Will and Tom came on to the house, saw Jack was gone.

Will says, "I reckon that's the last of Jack. I'll bet ye a dollar Old Fire Dragaman's done took him off and eat him. Dinner's still on the table."

So they sat down and went on eatin'. Jack came on in directly.

Will says, "Where'n the world ye been, Jack? We 'lowed Old Fire Dragaman had done eat ye up."

"I been watchin' where Old Fire Dragaman went to."

"How come dinner yet on the table?"

"I tried my best to get him to eat," says Jack. "He just lit his old pipe and went on back. I follered him, saw him go down in a big hole out yonder."

"You right sure ye ain't lyin', Jack?"

"Why, no," says Jack. "You boys come with me and you can see the place where he went in at. Let us get a rope and basket so we can go in that hole and see what's down there."

So they got a big basket made out of splits, and gathered up a long rope they'd done made out of hickory bark, and Jack took 'em on down to Old Fire Dragaman's den.

"Will, you're the oldest," says Jack; "we'll let you go down first. If you see any danger you shake the rope and we'll pull ye back up."

Will got in the basket, says, "You recollect now; whenever I shake that rope, you pull me out of here in a hurry."

So they let him down. Directly the rope shook, they jerked the basket back out, says, "What'd ye see, Will?"

"Saw a big house. Hit's like another world down there."

Then they slapped Tom in the basket and let him down; the rope shook, they hauled him up.

"What'd you see, Tom?"

"Saw a house and the barn."

Then they got Jack in the basket, and let him down. Jack got down on top of the house, let the basket slip down over the eaves and right on down in the yard. Jack got out, went and knocked on the door.

The prettiest girl Jack ever had seen came out. He started right in to courtin' her, says, "I'm goin' to get you out of here."

She says, "I got another sister in the next room yonder, prettier'n me. You get her out too."

So Jack went on in the next room. That second girl was a heap prettier'n the first, and Jack went to talkin' to her and was a-courtin' right on. Said he'd get her out of that place.

She says, "I got another sister in the next room, prettier'n me. Don't you want to get her out too?"

"Well, I didn't know they got any prettier'n you," says Jack, "but I'll go see."

So he went on in. Time Jack saw that 'un he knowed she was the prettiest girl ever lived, so he started in right off talkin' courtin' talk to her; plumb forgot about them other two.

That girl said to Jack, says, "Old Fire Dragaman'll be back here any minute now. Time he finds you here he'll start in spittin' balls of fire."

So she went and opened up an old chest, took out a big sword and a little vial of ointment, says, "If one of them balls of fire hits ye, Jack, you rub on a little of this medicine right quick, and this here sword is the only thing that will hurt Old Fire Dragaman. You watch out now, and kill him if ye can."

Well, the old giant came in the door directly, saw Jack, and com-menced spittin' balls of fire all around in there, some of 'em big as pumpkins. Jack he went a-dodgin' around tryin' to get at the old giant with that sword. Once in a while one of them fireballs 'uld glance him, but Jack rubbed on that ointment right quick and it didn't even make a blister. Fin'ly Jack got in close and clipped him with that sword, took his head clean off.

Then Jack made that girl promise she'd marry him. So she took a red ribbon and got Jack to plait it in her hair. Then she gave Jack a wishin' ring. He put it on his finger and they went on out and got the other two girls.

They were awful pleased. They told Jack they were such little bits of children when the old giant catched 'em they barely could recollect when they first came down there.

Well, Jack put the first one in the basket and shook the rope. Will and Tom hauled her up, and when they saw her they commenced fightin' right off to see which one would marry her.

She told 'em, says, "I got another sister down there."

"Is she any prettier'n you?" says Will.

She says to him, "I ain't sayin'."

Will and Tom chunked the basket back down in a hurry. Jack put the next girl in, shook the rope. Time Will and Tom saw her, they both asked her to marry, and went to knockin' and beatin' one another over gettin' *her*.

She stopped 'em, says, "We got one more sister down there."

"Is she prettier'n you?" says Will.

She says to him, "You can see for yourself."

So they slammed the basket back down, jerked that last girl out.

"Law me!" says Will. "This here's the one I'm a-goin' to marry."

"Oh, no, you ain't!" Tom says. "You'll marry me, won't ye now?"

"No," says the girl, "I've done promised to marry Jack."

"Blame Jack," says Will. "He can just stay in there." And he picked up the basket and rope, throwed 'em down the hole.

"There ain't nothin' much to eat down there," says the girl; "he'll starve to death."

"That's just what we want him to do," says Will, and they took them girls on back up to the house.

Well, Jack eat ever'thing he could find down there, but in about three days he saw the rations were runnin' awful low. He scrapped up ever' bit there was left and then he was plumb out of vittles; didn't know what he'd do.

In about a week Jack had com-menced to get awful poor. Happened he looked at his hand, turned that ring to see how much he'd fallen off, says, "I wish I was back home settin' in my mother's chimney corner smokin' my old chunky pipe."

And next thing, there he was.

Jack's mother asked him how come he wasn't up at the newground. Jack told her that was exactly where he was started.

When Jack got up there, Will and Tom were still a-fightin' over that youngest girl. Jack came on in the house and saw she still had that red ribbon in her hair, and she came over to him, says, "Oh Jack!"

So Jack got the youngest and Tom got the next 'un, and that throwed Will to take the oldest.

And last time I was down there they'd done built 'em three pole cabins and they were all doin' pretty well.

Tall Tales

Pecos Bill Becomes a Coyote

Pecos Bill had the strangest and most exciting experience any boy ever had. He became a member of a pack of wild Coyotes, and until he was a grown man, believed that his name was Cropear, and that he was a full-blooded Coyote. Later he discovered that he was a human being and very shortly thereafter became the greatest cowboy of all time. This is how it all came about.

Pecos Bill's family was migrating westward through Texas in the early days, in an old covered wagon with wheels made from cross sections of a sycamore log. His father and mother were riding in the front seat, and his father was driving a wall-eyed, spavined roan horse and a red and white spotted milch cow hitched side by side. The eighteen children in the back of the wagon were making such a medley of noises that their mother said it wasn't possible even to hear thunder.

Just as the wagon was rattling down to the ford across the Pecos River, the rear left wheel bounced over a great piece of rock, and Bill, his red hair bristling like porcupine quills, rolled out of the rear of the wagon, and landed, up to his neck, in a pile of loose sand. He was only four years old

169

at the time, and he lay dazed until the wagon had crossed the river and disappeared into the sage brush. It wasn't until his mother rounded up the family for the noonday meal that Bill was missed. The last anyone remembered seeing him was just before they had forded the river.

The mother and eight or ten of the older children hurried back to the river and hunted everywhere, but they could find no trace of the lost boy. When evening came, they were forced to go back to the covered wagon, and later, to continue their journey without him. Ever after, when they thought of Bill, they remembered the river, and so they naturally came to speak of him as Pecos Bill.

What had happened to Bill was this. He had strayed off into the mesquite,* and a few hours later was found by a wise old Coyote, who was the undisputed leader of the Loyal and Approved Packs of the Pecos and Rio Grande Valleys. He was, in fact, the Granddaddy of the entire race of Coyotes, and so his followers, out of affection to him, called him Grandy.

When he accidentally met Bill, Grandy was curious, but shy. He sniffed and he yelped, and he ran this way and that, the better to get the scent, and to make sure there was no danger. After a while he came quite near, sat up on his haunches, and waited to see what the boy would do. Bill trotted up to Grandy and began running his hands through the long shaggy hair.

"What a nice doggy you are," he repeated again and again.

"Yes, and what a nice Cropear you are," yelped Grandy joyously.

And so, ever after, the Coyotes called the child Cropear.

Grandy was much pleased with his find and so, by running ahead and stopping and barking softly, he led the boy to the jagged side of Cabezon, or the Big Head, as it was called. This was a towering mass of mountain that rose

*Spiny shrubs.

abruptly, as if by magic, from the prairie. Around the base of this mountain the various families of the Loyal and Approved Packs had burrowed out their dens.

Here, far away from the nearest human dwelling, Grandy made a home for Cropear, and taught him all the knowledge of the wild out-of-doors. He led Cropear to the berries that were good to eat, and dug up roots that were sweet and spicy. He showed the boy how to break open the small nuts from the piñon; and when Cropear wanted a drink, he led him to a vigorous young mother Coyote who gave him of her milk. Cropear thus drank in the very life blood of a thousand generations of wild life and became a native beast of the prairie, without at all knowing that he was a man-child.

Grandy became his teacher and schooled him in the knowledge that had been handed down through thousands of generations of the Pack's life. He taught Cropear the many signal calls, and the code of right and wrong, and the gentle art of loyalty to the leader. He also trained him to leap long distances and to dance; and to flip-flop and to twirl his body so fast that the eye could not follow his movements. And most important of all, he instructed him in the silent, rigid pose of invisibility, so that he could see all that was going on around him without being seen.

And Cropear grew tall and strong, he became the pet of the Pack. The Coyotes were always bringing him what they thought he would like to eat, and were ever showing him the many secrets of the fine art of hunting. They taught him where the Field-mouse nested, where the Song Thrush hid her eggs, where the Squirrel stored his nuts; and where the Mountain Sheep concealed their young among the towering rocks.

When the Jack-rabbit was to be hunted, they gave Cropear his station and taught him to do his turn in the relay race. And when the prong-horn Antelope was to be captured, Cropear took his place among the

171

encircling pack and helped bring the fleeting animal to bay and pull him down, in spite of his darting, charging antlers.

Grandy took pains to introduce Cropear to each of the animals and made every one of them promise he would not harm the growing man-child. "Au-g-gh!" growled the Mountain Lion, "I will be as careful as I can. But be sure to tell your child to be careful, too!"

"Gr-r-rr!" growled the fierce Grizzly Bear, "I have crunched many a marrow bone, but I will not harm your boy. Gr-r-rr!"

"Yes we'll keep our perfumery and our quills in our inside vest pockets," mumbled the silly Skunk and Porcupine, as if suffering from adenoids.

But when Grandy talked things over with the Bull Rattlesnake, he was met with the defiance of hissing rattles. "Nobody will ever make me promise to protect anybody or anything! S-s-s-s-ss! I'll do just as I please!"

"Be careful of your wicked tongue," warned Grandy, "or you'll be very sorry."

But when Grandy met the Wouser, things were even worse. The Wouser was a cross between the Mountain Lion and the Grizzly Bear, and was ten times larger than either. Besides that, he was the nastiest creature in the world. "I can only give you fair warning," yowled the Wouser, "and if you prize your man-child, as you say you do, you will have to keep him out of harm's way!" And as the Wouser continued, he stalked back and forth, lashing his tail and gnashing his jaws, and acting as if he were ready to snap somebody's head off. "What's more, you know that nobody treats me as a friend. Everybody runs around behind my back spreading lies about me. Everybody says I carry hydrophobia—the deadly poison—about on my person, and because of all these lies, I am shunned like a leper. Now you come sneaking around asking me to help you. Get out of my sight before I do something I shall be sorry for!"

"I'm not sneaking," barked Grandy in defiance, "and besides, you're the one who will be sorry in the end."

So it happened that all the animals, save only the Bull Rattlesnake and the Wouser, promised to help Cropear bear a charmed life so that no harm should come near him. And by good fortune, the boy was never sick. The vigorous exercise and the fresh air and the constant sunlight helped him to become the healthiest, strongest, most active boy in the world.

When Pecos Bill, the Coyotes' *Cropear*, met Chuck, a cowpuncher, and discovered that he was human, he learned to speak and joined Chuck's company of cowpunchers at the I. X. L. Ranch.

Babe the Blue Ox

Paul Bunyan couldn't of done all the great loggin' he did if it hadn't been for Babe the Blue Ox. I believe I mentioned helpin' to take care of him for a couple of months when I first come to camp, and then I helped measure him once afterwards for a new yoke Ole had to make for him. He'd broke the one he had when Paul was doin' an extra quick job haulin' lumber for some millmen down in Muskegon one summer, and Ole had to make him a new one right away and so we had to take Babe's measurements.

I've forgot most of the other figgurs, but I remember he measured forty-two axhandles between the eyes—and a tobacco box—you could easy fit in a Star tobacco box after the last axhandle. That tobacco box was lost and we couldn't never take the measurements again, but I remember that's what it was. And he weighed accordin'. Though he never was weighed that I know of, for there never was any scales made that would of been big enough.

Paul told Ole he might as well make him a new log chain

too while he was at it, for the way Babe pulled on 'em, in just about a month or two what had been a chain would be pulled out into a solid bar and wouldn't be any good. And so we measured him up for the chain too.

Babe was so long in the body, Paul used to have to carry a pair of field glasses around with him so as he could see what he was doin' with his hind feet.

One time Babe kicked one of the straw bosses in the head so his brains all run out, but the cook happened to be handy and he filled up the hole with hotcake batter and plastered it together again and he was just as good as ever. And right now, if I'm not mistaken, that boss is runnin' camp for the Bigham Loggin' Company of Virginia, Minnesota.

Babe was so big that every time they shod him they had to open up a new iron mine on Lake Superior, and one time when Ole the Blacksmith carried one of his shoes a mile and a half he sunk a foot and a half in solid rock at every step.

His color was blue—a fine, pretty, deep blue—and that's why he was called the Blue Ox—when you looked up at him the air even looked blue all around him. His nose was pretty near all black, but red on the inside, of course, and he had big white horns, curly on the upper section—about the upper third—and kind of darkish brown at the tip, and then the rest of him was all that same deep blue.

He didn't use to be always that blue color though. He was white when he was a calf. But he turned blue standin' out in the field for six days the first winter of the Blue Snow, and he never got white again. Winter and summer he was always the same, except probly in July—somewheres about the Fourth—he might maybe've been a shade lighter then.

I've heard some of the old loggers say that Paul brought him from Canada when he was a little calf a few days old—carried him across Lake Champlain in a sack so he wouldn't have to pay duty on him. But I'm thinkin' he must of been a mighty few days old at the time or Paul couldn't of done it, for he must of grown pretty fast when he got started, to grow to the size he did. And then besides there's them that says Paul never had him at all when he was a little fellow like that, but that he was a pretty fair-sized calf when Paul got him. A fellow by the name of O'Regan down near Detroit is supposed to of had him first. O'Regan didn't have no more'n about forty acres or so under cultivation cleared on his farm and naturally that wasn't near enough to raise feed for Babe, and so he's supposed to of sold him the year of the Short Oats to Paul Bunyan. I don't know exactly. It's all before my time. When I went to work for Paul, and all the time I knowed him, the Ox was full grown.

Babe was as strong as the breath of a tote-teamster, Paul always said, and he could haul a whole section of timber with him at a time—Babe'd walk right off with it—the entire six hundred forty acres at one drag, and haul it down to the landin' and dump it in. That's why there ain't no section thirty-seven* no more. Six trips a day six days a week just cleaned up a township, and the last load they never bothered to haul back Saturday night, but left it lay on the landin' to float away in the spring, and that's why there quit bein' section 37's, and you never see 'em on the maps no more.

The only time I ever saw Babe on a job that seemed to nearly stump him—but sure did look like it was goin' to for a while, though—durin' all the time I was with Paul was one time in Wisconsin, down on the St. Croix. And that was when he used him to pull the crooks out of eighteen miles of loggin' road; that come pretty near bein' more'n the Ox could handle. For generally anything that had two ends to it Babe could walk off with like nothin'.

But that road of all the crooked roads I ever see—and I've seen a good many in my day—was of all of 'em the

* When new land was being settled, each township consisted of thirty-six land grants or sections. "Section thirty-seven", therefore, never existed.

crookedest, and it's no wonder it was pretty near too much for Babe. You won't believe me when I tell you, but it's the truth, that in that stretch of eighteen miles that road doubled back on itself no less than sixteen times, and made four figure 8's, nine 3's, and four S's, yes, and one each of pretty near every other letter in the alphabet.

Of course the trouble with that road was, there was too much of it, and it didn't know what to do with itself, and so it's no wonder it got into mischief.

You'd be walkin' along it, all unsuspectin', and here of a sudden you'd see a coil of it layin' behind a tree, that you never know'd was there, and layin' there lookin' like it was ready to spring at you. The teamsters met themselves comin' back so many times while drivin' over it, that it begun to get on their nerves and we come near havin' a crazy-house in camp there. And so Paul made up his mind that that there road was goin' to be straightened out right then and there, and he went after it accordin'.

What he done was, he went out and told Bill to bring up the Blue Ox right away, and hitch him to the near end of the road.

Then he went up and spoke somethin' kind of low to Babe, and then afterwards he went out kind of one side himself, and Babe laid hold, and then is the time it come pretty near breakin' the Ox in two, like I said.

"Come on, Babe! Co-ome on, Ba-abe!" says Paul, and the Ox lays hold and pulls to the last ounce of him. If I live to be a hundred years old I never hope to see an ox pull like that again. His hind legs laid straight out behind him nearly, and his belly was almost down touchin' the ground.

It was one beeg job, as the Frenchmen would of said. And when the crooks finally was all out of that there piece of road, there was enough of it to lay around a round lake we skidded logs into that winter, and then there was enough left in the place where it'd been at first to reach from one end to the other.

I've always been glad I saw Babe on that pull, for it's the greatest I ever saw him do—in its way, anyway.

Bill, that took care of the Blue Ox, generally went by the name of Brimstone Bill at camp and the reason was because he got to be so awfully red-hot tempered. But I never blamed him, though. Havin' that Ox to take care of was enough to make a sinner out of the best fellow that ever lived. Of all the scrapin' and haulin' you'd have to do to keep him lookin' anywheres near respectable even, no one would ever think.

And the way he ate—it took two men just to pick the balin' wire out of his teeth at mealtimes. Four ton of grain wasn't nothin' for Babe to get away with at a single meal, and for the hay—I can't mention quantities, but I know they said at first, before he got Windy Knight onto cuttin' it up for nails to use in puttin' on the cook-house roof, Paul used to have to move the camp every two weeks to get away from the mess of haywire that got collected where Babe ate his dinner. And as for cleanin' the barn and haulin' the manure away—

I remember one night in our bunkhouse as plain as if it'd been yesterday. I can see it all again just like it was then. That was one time afterwards, when we was loggin' down in Wisconsin.

There was a new fellow just come to camp that day, a kind of college fellow that'd come to the woods for his health, and we was all sittin' around the stove that night spinnin' yarns like we almost always done of an evenin' while our socks was dryin'. I was over on one end, and to each side of me was Joe Stiles, and Pat O'Henry—it's funny how I remember it all—and a fellow by the name of Horn, and Big Gus, and a number of others that I don't recollect now, and over on the other end opposite me was Brimstone Bill, and up by me was this new fellow, but kind of a little to the side.

Well, quite a number of stories had been told, and some of 'em had been about the Blue Ox and different experi-

ences men'd had with him different times and how the
manure used to pile up, and pretty soon that there college
chap begun to tell a story he said it reminded him of—one
of them there old ancient Greek stories, he said it was,
about Herukles cleanin' the Augaen stables, that was one
of twelve other hard jobs he'd been set to do by the king he
was workin' for at the time, to get his daughter or somethin' like that. He was goin' at it kind of fancy, describin'
how the stables hadn't been cleaned for some time, and
what a condition they was in as a consequence, and what a
strong man Herukles was, and how he adopted the plan of
turnin' the river right through the stables and so washin'
the manure away that way, and goin' on describin' how it
was all done. And how the water come through and floated
the manure all up on top of the river, and how there was
enough of it to spread over a whole valley, and then how
the manure rolled up in waves again in the river when it got
to where it was swifter—and it was a pretty good story and
he was quite a talker too, that young fellow was, and he
had all the men listenin' to him.

Well, all the time old Brimstone Bill he sat there takin' it
all in, and I could see by the way his jaw was workin' on his
tobacco that he was gettin' pretty riled. Everythin' had
been quiet while the young fellow was tellin' the story, and
some of us was smokin', some of us enjoyin' a little fresh
Star or Peerless maybe and spittin' in the sandbox
occasionally which was gettin' pretty wet by this time, and
there wasn't no sound at all except the occasional sizzle
when somebody hit the stove, or the movin' of a bench
when somebody's foot or sock would get too near the fire,
and the man's voice goin' along describin' about this
Herukles and how great he was and how fine the stables
looked when he got through with 'em, when all at once
Brimstone Bill he busted right into him:

"You shut your blamed mouth about that Herik Lees of
yourn," he says. "I guess if your Herik Lees had had the
job I've got for a few days, he wouldn't of done it so easy or

talked so smart, you young Smart Alec, you—" and then a long string of 'em the way Bill could roll 'em off when he got mad—I never heard any much better'n him—they said he could keep goin' for a good half hour and never repeat the same word twict—but I wouldn't give much for a lumberjack who couldn't roll off a few dozen straight—specially if he's worked with cattle—and all the time he was gettin' madder'n madder till he was fairly sizzlin' he was so mad. "I guess if that Mr. Lees had had Babe to take care of he wouldn't of done it so easy. Tell him he can trade jobs with me for a spell if he wants to, and see how he likes it. I guess if he'd of had to use his back on them one hundred and fifty jacks to jack up the barn the way I got to do he wouldn't of had enough strength left in him to brag so much about it. I just got through raisin' it another sixty foot this afternoon. When this job started we was workin' on the level, and now already Babe's barn is up sixteen hundred foot. I'd like to see the river that could wash that pile of manure away, and you can just tell that Herik Lees to come on and try it if he wants to. And if he can't, why, then you can just shut up about it. I've walked the old Ox and cleaned 'im and doctored 'im and rubbed 'im ever since he was first invented, and I know what it is, and I ain't goin' to sit here and let you tell me about any Mr. Lees or any other blankety blank liar that don't know what he's talkin' about tellin' about cleanin' barns—not if I know it." And at it he goes again blankety blank blank all the way out through the door, and slams it behind him so the whole bunkhouse shook, and the stranger he sits there and don't know hardly what to make of it. Till I kind of explained to him afterwards before we turned in, and we all, the rest of 'em too, told him not to mind about Bill, for he couldn't hardly help it. After he'd been in camp a few days he'd know. You couldn't hardly blame Bill for bein' aggravated—used to be a real good-natured man, and he wasn't so bad even that time I was helpin' him, but the Ox was too much for any man, no matter who.

181

And so I never held it against Bill much myself. He was fond of Babe too and made quite a pet of him, more so than the rest of us even, and we all did.

"I been with the beast a good long time," he used to say, "and I know the cantankerous old reptile most the same's if I had been through him with a lantern. I know how to do for 'im, and all his little ways and all, and I don't want anybody else botherin' round and messin' things up for me. I can take care of 'im all right. All I want is to be let alone."

Afterwards when Paul got his hay farm down in Wisconsin it made it easier for Bill. Then we'd just rake the hay up in windrows and let it freeze that way layin' out across the fields, and in the winter they'd haul it in one end first in the stable and cut it up in chunks for Babe, just pullin' it up a little each time. That way you could get away from the nuisance of the haywire, and didn't have that to bother with.

In any of his small camps Paul couldn't never keep Babe but a day or so at a time, because it took the tote-teamsters a year to haul a day's feed for him.

Babe was a kind of playful fellow too. Sometimes he'd step in a river and lay down there and so make the water rise and leave a boom of logs that was below there up high and dry, and again sometimes he'd step on a ridge makin' a lakeshore maybe, and smash it down and let out the water to flood a river and drown out some low water drive.

Around the camp he'd play with almost any of us who was willin' to play with him after the day's work. We used to feed him hotcakes sometimes and he got awful fond of 'em. Them big ones we made on the big griddle we used to fold up in quarters and put clover hay in between and give it to him for a sandwich and he liked that powerful well. But we shouldn't of done it, I know that now. I've thought many times since, it's too bad, for that's what got him started, and once started he seemed he couldn't never stop. Poor old Babe. It proved to be the death of him at last.

It was all wrong of us, but of course, we didn't think about it then, and had no notion what it would lead to in the end.

Paul Bunyan was sure fond of his Ox, and mighty proud of him too, as he'd a right to be.

"Be faithful," he used to say to him low under his breath as he walked along beside him. "Be faithful, my Babe. Faithful."

Stormalong Fights the Kraken

Unique among tall-tale heroes in America was Alfred Bull-top Stormalong. Like those outsized figures, Paul Bunyan and Pecos Bill, he belonged to the tradition, being a giant himself, with imagination and a gift for invention. But he was not just a North American. He came to know the world, for he was a seaman. In the merchant marine he worked on the *Lady of the Sea* in the China trade. Later, after he had served as first mate on the *Lady of the Sea*, and had taken some time out to work on the land, his men built a ship for him, as a present and a surprise. She was an immense ship, as long as the arm of Cape Cod itself, designed to tempt him back to the sea, and she was named the *Tuscarora*.

On one of her voyages she was threatened with destruction three times within a matter of days. Returning from a routine run to Capetown, she was ordered to stop at Stockholm in the Baltic Sea for a cargo of pickled herring.

Stormalong examined his charts carefully. He realized that the run might involve a tight squeeze in the Kattegat, that narrow strait of water between Denmark and Sweden. Some of his officers, moreover, were alarmed by the reports of the giant kraken, a mysterious under-water beast which was said to live in the waters off the coast of Norway.

The giant kraken is related to the octopus. He is, in fact, one of the few remaining examples of a pre-historic branch of the family. In shape he vaguely resembles a crab, with a hard, armored shell a mile and a half in circumference over the mass of his body. This shell is of a mottled dark green which blends with the dark green of deep sea water. He is practically invisible, even to the trained eyes of Scandinavian sailors. His great tentacles, like giant lobster claws, extend from the sides of the shell. He is not a pretty beast.

His habits are even less attractive than his appearance. Although he lives at the bottom of the sea, eighty to one hundred fathoms below the surface, he likes to vary his diet with such delicacies as flocks of sea-gulls and fishing dories with their crews. At unpredictable intervals he rises to the surface to indulge himself in these dainties. Whenever he rises, the water swirls and eddies for miles around, like shoal water. When he submerges, the suction creates a tremendous whirlpool that can pull large ships down into seething destruction.

Out in the open waters of the North Sea, where uncharted shoals give warning that the kraken is active, there is not too much danger. A fast ship can change course in time to sail around the critical area. In a narrow body of water like the Kattegat, however, the kraken can be difficult indeed.

Stormalong listened to the tales his officers had to tell and thought about the matter. He himself had often heard tales of its existence. He recalled other terrors of the sea, however, which he had overcome. Among them he recalled his fight with the octopus in the West Indies. He had been hardly more than a boy when that took place! He thought, too, about his wild ride across the Pacific on the back of a great white whale. No serious damage had come of that!

185

On the basis of these recollections and with the knowledge that the *Tuscarora* was the most manageable ship afloat, he decided not to worry about the kraken. He had, furthermore, set his heart on a good breakfast of pickled herring! He ordered the course set for Stockholm!

The *Tuscarora* had just passed the great beacon of the Naze when queer things began to happen. Whirlpools and eddies appeared for no good reason in the deepest water of the channel. A rip tide caught the ship and almost whirled her around, while a gust of wind threatened to drive her on the rocks of the Norwegian coast. Stormalong kept the wheel firmly in hand. The *Tuscarora* stubbornly held to her course. The Bosun was frightened as he took his soundings. He was well acquainted with these waters, and knew that the channel should be fifty fathoms deep. Each time a whirlpool appeared, however, the water grew more shallow.

"Twenty fathoms," he sang out, "eighteen fathoms . . . fifteen fathoms . . . twelve fathoms . . .!" The pitch of his voice grew higher with each announcement. Stormalong chuckled to himself. He knew that he had met the kraken and that the *Tuscarora* was equal to the situation.

"All hands on deck!" he shouted. "Get up the topmast stuns'ls! Crowd the canvas on her! What she can't carry, she'll have to drag!"

The crew sprang to the rigging. The *Tuscarora* leaped through the water, her slim bow slipping through the choppy sea like a snake through a stand of grasses. Then, as a well-trained hunter jumps over a wall, the *Tuscarora* cleared the back of the kraken and settled herself in the calm water of the channel.

She made a ninety-degree turn as Stormalong quickly flipped the wheel and headed her around the Skaw, the pointed tip of Denmark which separates the Skagerrak from the Kattegat. The impetus of the dash over the kraken's back carried the ship through the straits of Elsinore. She was safely at anchor off Stockholm by the next morning.

Stormalong spent a pleasant evening in Stockholm recounting his adventures to a pair of Swedish captains whom he had met on visits to the Chinese ports. These men were much interested in the story. They assured Stormalong that few ships had been as lucky as the *Tuscarora*.

In addition to the twenty thousand barrels of pickled herring, Stormy took on a load of Swedish steel, which he happened to pick up at a bargain. The *Tuscarora* rode low in the water under the weight of her cargo as she set out on her return from Stockholm. The Captain himself kept the wheel to carry her past the narrow waters of the Kattegat and out into the feeding grounds of the kraken. They had just cleared the Skagerrak when the first evidence of the lurking beast appeared. The ground swell broke into whitecaps, the waters swirled with an ominous rhythm, and the Bosun's soundings showed shoal water where no shoals were charted. The Captain prepared to use the same tactics he had used successfully once before. He was about to order all hands aloft when the wind died.

Stormalong had not counted upon this. The swirling of the waters slowed to a lazy pace. This was proof that the kraken was aware of the dying of the wind. The *Tuscarora* was becalmed directly above the back of the monster and completely at its mercy!

The Bosun shrieked his soundings frantically. "Ten fathoms! . . . Lord have mercy! . . . Eight fathoms! . . . Seven fathom! . . . Six fathoms! . . . Save us!" He begged the Captain to throw the steel overboard in the hopes that the ship would ride more lightly and be able to get away.

Stormalong was well aware of the dangers immediately ahead. He blamed himself for being overconfident. He should have listened more carefully to his friends the Swedish captains. Better still, he should not have attempted the trip in the first place. The *Tuscarora* was a ship for the open ocean. Penned up in a little sea, she could not maneuver freely. His thoughtless pride had placed her and

187

all her loyal crew in jeopardy. It was up to him to get her out of the difficulty.

Stormy carefully checked the distance between the whirlpools on the surface of the water. He checked the Bosun's soundings and the color of the sea. He figured that the neck of the kraken lay half a mile ahead and would soon emerge. There was only one chance to take, and he was the only one who could take it.

He stripped off his coat and his cap and leaped to the foc's'le. "Open the gear locker!" he shouted to the Mate. "Break out the biggest harpoon we carry!"

The heavy iron was dragged forward and Stormy coiled the line at his feet. He braced himself and kept his eyes on the horizon. Just as he had guessed, an ugly snout broke through the water half a mile in front of the ship's bow, spouting contemptuously into the air. Stormy's eyes narrowed with anger when the monster challenged him to the duel. His huge right arm swung back in a great arc, then forward. The harpoon whistled through the air and buried itself in the kraken's neck.

"All hands aloft! Prepare to crowd sail!" roared Stormalong, as the kraken recovered from the shock. The monster writhed and wriggled, lashed his tentacles. He tried to shaked off the harpoon and fling the ship against the cliffs of Stavanger. But Stormalong held on. In a last desperate effort, the kraken dove into the depths.

Stormy had been waiting for this. The watery walls of the great funnel which opened behind the kraken whirled at a tremendous speed. The *Tuscarora* raced around the edge of the crater, barely keeping its balance. Slowly and carefully, Stormy played out the line of the harpoon until at last he let it go entirely. The ship shot off the crater from the centrifugal force of its whirling and cleared the treacherous area of the whirlpool. The sailors quickly unfurled the canvas, just in time to catch a fresh breeze, and the *Tuscarora*, safe again, settled in the bosom of the North Sea. It had been a close call, but Stormalong had saved the day!

The crew felt that there had been enough excitement for one voyage. But the *Tuscarora's* troubles were not over. The fresh breeze died suddenly. A fog blanketed the ocean. Usually a fog at sea is accompanied by calm water, but not this one. The North Sea heaved and tossed alarmingly as the death throes of the kraken made themselves felt.

Meanwhile the fog grew worse and worse. It was so thick the men had to cut paths with axes in order to reach their stations. It was impossible to tell where the fog ended and the sea began. Even the fish were confused. One of the junior officers ran headlong into a school of deep-sea bass, who had lost their way and were swimming blindly on the afterdeck. When Hammerhead went below after his watch, he found a family of mackerel snuggled comfortably in his bunk.

At last the fog cleared. The *Tuscarora* had indeed worked herself into a tight spot. She had been swept into the narrow end of the North Sea, between England and Holland. As luck would have it, she was heading southwest by west. Directly ahead of her loomed the Straits of Dover.

At their narrowest, between Folkestone and Calais, the Straits measure about twenty miles wide. This was roughly the width of the *Tuscarora* amidships. There was obviously no room in which the ship could be turned around in order to leave the North Sea through the open waters north of Scotland. The prevailing wind was north-northeast. Any effort to back the ship into a wider channel would be unsuccessful. Stormalong called a conference of all his officers.

The meeting in the Captain's cabin was short. When the men emerged, Stormy gave an order to drop anchor and put the lifeboats over the port side. The officers retired to their cabins, and quickly returned to the deck in their best dress uniforms. Five thousand barrels of pickled herrings were lowered into the lifeboats along with the officers. The little fleet headed for The Hague on the Dutch shore.

As everyone knows, the Dutch are among the cleanest

and tidiest people on earth. In order to keep their houses shining and their faces glistening, they need soap—and plenty of it! They are also very fond of pickled herring.

Stormalong's officers went straight to the town hall and explained their predicament to the city fathers. The good Dutch burghers listened sympathetically. They were, for the most part, merchants and seafaring men themselves. They had long known and admired the reputation of Captain Stormalong and were happy to help him in his hour of need. At first they refused the gift of pickled herring. But they were finally persuaded to accept it.

Couriers were sent to every nook and corner of Holland, and to a few selected border towns in Belgium. Everywhere housewives opened their cupboards and gave up their stores of soap. Delicately perfumed face soap, harsh scrubbing soap, laundry soap, shaving soap, and even scouring powder, were loaded into dogcarts and trundled to the boats waiting in the harbor of The Hague. The coast of Holland was jammed with sightseers, who came with their families and picnic baskets to watch the operation.

Once the soap had been taken aboard the *Tuscarora*, Stormy put the men to work. The crew were let down over the sides in bosun's chairs, each man with a brush and a bucket of soap jelly. They spread the soap as thick as they could over the hull. At the end of a long day's work, the *Tuscarora* was smeared from stem to stern with a slippery coating. Little froths of suds, like a lace edging, encircled her water-line.

When the work was completed, Stormalong ordered the anchor hauled up, the canvas unfurled. Taking advantage of a brisk wind, he urged the ship forward into the narrow straits. It was a tight squeeze! The picnicking Dutchmen on the shore joined the crew in a loud cheer as the *Tuscarora* slipped through the narrow bottle-neck and cleared her way into the English Channel out onto the broad Atlantic.

Phew! said Stormy to himself, as he realized he was at last headed home after an eventful voyage.

The choppy waters of the Channel washed a good bit of the soap off the ship's sides. For weeks thereafter clouds of iridescent soap bubbles rose into the sky like round rainbows whenever the wind freshened. Bubbles are temporary things at best, however, and in time these were forgotten.

One permanent souvenir of the incident remained. As the *Tuscarora* squeezed through the narrowest channel, her starboard rail brushed against the cliffs on the British coast. The soap on that side was scraped off by the jutting rocks. To this day it remains there. It stands out white and clear, and has become a famous landmark for tourists. The headlands, which had before been a sandy red, were now the color of chalk. They have been known since as the White Cliffs of Dover.

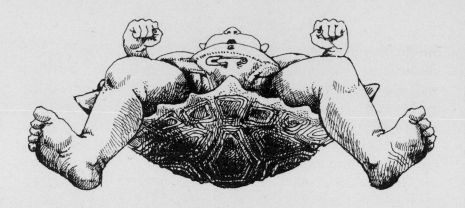

Strong but Quirky

The morning Davy Crockett was born Davy's Pa came busting out of his cabin in Tennessee alongside the Nola-chucky River. He fired three shots into the air, gave a whoop, and said, "I've got me a son. His name is Davy Crockett, and he'll be the greatest hunter in all creation."

When he said that the sun rose up in the sky like a ball of fire. The wind howled riproariously. Thunder boomed, and all the critters and varmints of the forest let out a moan.

Then Davy's Pa went back into the cabin. Little Davy was stretched out in a cradle made of a snapping turtle's shell. There was a pair of elk horns over the top, and over the elk horns was the skin of a wildcat. The cradle was run by water power, and it was rocking away—rockety-whump, rockety-whump.

Now all the Crocketts were big, but Davy was big even for a Crockett. He weighed two hundred pounds, fourteen ounces, and he was as frisky as a wildcat. His Ma and his Aunt Ketinah stood over Davy, trying to get him to sleep.

"Sing somethin' to quiet the boy," said Aunt Ketinah to his Uncle Roarious, who was standing in a corner combing his hair with a rake.

Uncle Roarious opened his mouth and sang a bit of *Over*

the River to Charley. That is, it was meant for singing. It sounded worse than a nor'easter howling around a country barn at midnight.

"Hmmm," said Uncle Roarious. He reached for a jug and took him a sip of kerosene oil to loosen up his pipes.

Davy was sitting up in his cradle. He kept his peepers on his uncle, watching him pull at the jug.

"I'll have a sip o' the same," said Davy, as loud as you please.

That kerosene jug slipped right out of Uncle Roarious's hand. Davy's Ma and his Aunt Ketinah let out a shriek.

"Why, the little shaver can talk!" said Davy's Pa.

"We-el," said Davy, talking slow and easy-like, "maybe I don't jabber good enough to make a speech in Congress, but I reckon I got the hang of 'er. It's nothin' to Davy Crockett."

"That's mighty big talk, Son," said Davy's Pa.

"It ought to be," said Davy. "It's comin' from a big man."

And with that he leaped out of his cradle, kicked his heels together, and crowed like a rooster. He flapped his arms and he bellowed, "I'm Davy Crockett, fresh from the backwoods! I'm half horse, half alligator, with a little touch o' snappin' turtle! I can wade the Mississippi, ride a streak o' lightnin', hug a bear too close for comfort, and whip my weight in wildcats! I can out-eat, out-sleep, out-fight, out-shoot, out-run, out-jump, and out-squat any man in these here United States! And I will!"

Aunt Ketinah eyed him as if he was a little bit of a mosquito making a buzz.

"That'll be enough o' your sass," said she, kind of sharp-like. "Now get back into your cradle and behave."

"Yes, ma'am," said Davy. He was always polite to the ladies.

"No such thing!" said Uncle Roarious. "Settin' in the cradle won't grow him none! We've got to plant him in the earth and water him with wild buffalo's milk, with boiled corncobs and tobacco leaves mixed in."

"Can't do any harm," said Davy's Ma.

"Might do good," said Davy's Pa.

"Suits me," said Davy. "Let's give 'er a try."

So they took Davy out to Thunder Shower Hill and planted him in the earth. They watered him with wild buffalo's milk, with boiled corncobs and tobacco leaves mixed in. The sun shone on him by day, and the moon beamed down on him by night. The wind cooled him and the rain freshened him. And Davy Crockett began to grow proper.

One morning Davy's Pa got up as usual and looked out the window. Instead of the sun shining, it was like a cloudy night with fog and no moon. Davy's Pa had never seen it so dark in all his born days.

"Hurricane's comin' up," he said to Uncle Roarious, who was standing in a corner buttoning up his cast-iron shirt.

"We'd better water Davy before she breaks," said Uncle Roarious.

Davy's Pa and Uncle Roarious each picked up a barrel of wild buffalo's milk, with boiled corncobs and tobacco leaves mixed in. Davy's Ma and Aunt Ketinah followed along, carrying another barrel between them.

But when they got outside there wasn't a sign of a hurricane. There wasn't any hurricane at all. The sky was blue with little white clouds, and the sun was shining just as pretty. Only reason it was dark was that Davy's shadow was falling over the cabin.

"Davy must have growed some," said Davy's Ma, and they all hurried over to Thunder Shower Hill. Davy was standing on tiptoe with his head poked through a cloud. He was taller than the tallest tree and a sight friskier.

Uncle Roarious let out a yip and Davy leaned down. Davy wiped a bit of cloud out of his eye and said, "I've been lookin' over the country. She's right pretty, and I think I'm goin' to like 'er."

"You'd better," said Aunt Ketinah, kind of snappy-like. "She's the only one you've got."

"Yes, ma'am!" roared out Davy. His voice was so loud it started an avalanche at Whangdoodle Knob, thirty miles away. The trees all around flattened out, and Aunt Ketinah, Uncle Roarious, and Davey's Ma and Pa fell over from the force of it.

Davy's Pa picked himself up and shook his head.

"He's too big," he said.

"Oh, I don't know," said Uncle Roarious. "He'll settle some."

"No," said Davy's Pa, "he's too big for a hunter. It wouldn't be fair and square."

"What are we goin' to do?" asked Uncle Roarious.

"Only one thing *to* do," said Davy's Pa. "We've got to uproot him and let him grow down to man-size."

So Davey's Ma and Pa, his Aunt Ketinah and his Uncle Roarious uprooted Davy. Soon as his feet were free, Davy leaped high into the air. He kicked his heels together, flapped his arms, and he bellowed, "Look out, all you critters and varmints o' the forest! For here comes Davy Crockett, fresh from the backwoods! I'm half horse, half alligator, with a little touch o' snappin' turtle! I can run faster, jump higher, squat lower, dive deeper, stay under water longer, and come up drier than any man in these here United States! Who-o-o-o-o-p!"

Uncle Roarious listened to Davy and he looked at Davy. Then he said, "He's strong, but he's quirky."

Davy's Pa looked at Davy and he listened to Davy.

"He'll do," he said. "He'll do for a Crockett till a better one comes along."

And when Davy's Pa said that, lightning flashed and thunder boomed. The wind howled riproariously, and all the critters and varmints of the forest let out a moan.

Johnny Appleseed

The next fellow I'm going to tell about in this history of America may or may not be a hero. There are good points to be made on both sides of the question. This fellow, name of Jonathan Chapman (or Johnny Appleseed) never fought anybody rough-and-tumble, never killed any whales or varmints, the way Stormy and Mike and Davy did. Fact is, he made it a point never to hurt a fly. Another thing, he wasn't smart like old Stormy and the others. Some claim that he was crazy as a coot—maybe a little crazier, and there may be something in what they say.

Still there are some people that set their jaws and say: "There wasn't anything gaudy about him, I'll agree. But he was a hero anyhow." And when you think of what this little rascal did, in spite of all his handicaps, you see that there are reasons for agreeing with these people.

Johnny Chapman was born about the time old Stormy made his first trip to sea. About the time Mike Fink took his first keelboat trip, Johnny found his calling, and he stuck to that line of work a good many years after Davy unfroze the frozen sun down in Tennessee.

196

Back there in Massachusetts on the day Johnny was born, there was one of those Massachusetts May storms that rain cats and a fair number of dogs. But along about when Baby Johnny had polished off his first big cry, the sun came out and made a handsome rainbow.

One end of this rainbow was hitched to Monadnock Hill, where the great carbuncle sparkled in the sunshine. From here the rainbow arched up in the gray-blue sky until the other end swooped down right smack into the Chapman dooryard near Ipswich. There, this end of the rainbow got all tangled up in a big Spitzenberger apple tree which was so loaded with blossoms that it looked more or less like a big snowball. Result was the rainbow colored up the blossoms with all the colors you can think of, off hand, at any rate.

The nurse that was taking care of Johnny and his mother claimed that she picked him up and carried him over to the window for a look at the tree.

"You'll never believe the way he carried on," she said. "Why, he humped and gurgled and stuck out his little white paws as if he wanted to pick all those blossoms! And he was only forty minutes old too!"

Well, frankly, some of us historians *don't* believe this story—sounds fishy to us. But it's a known fact that as long as Johnny was a baby, each spring he'd whoop and squall and holler around, not giving the family a lick of peace, until they handed him a branch of apple blossoms to hang onto. Then he wouldn't bang the petals off, or eat them, like other babies would. Instead, he'd just lie there in his crib, looking at those apple blossoms, sniffing at them now and then, and smiling as happy as an angel plumb full of ice cream.

When Johnny ended his babyhood and started in being a boy, his mother got to feeling that he was concentrating a little too much on apple trees. "Sonny," she said, "You've got to branch out a little. Apple blossoms are fine things, I agree. But you can't depend on them for all the joy you get out of life. Wild flowers and animals, in some ways, are more or less like apple blossoms, and you might come to like them, too. Come on and see."

So she'd take the little fellow and meander around in the woods with him, introducing him to plants and squirrels and such. Since she was part Indian (Pequod, I believe), Mrs. Chapman knew many of these things almost as well as she knew her kinfolk. And after a while, when Johnny had caught on, there wasn't anything that gave him as much pleasure as taking a stance in front of a wild flower or forest animal and just standing there to admire it until dinner time.

If a flower or weed had a name for making a body well, he'd just about go wild the minute he set eyes on it. Hoarhound, catnip, pennyroyal, ginseng, dog fennel— these were the growing things he favored above all others. Some of these things were as ugly as sin and smelled to high heaven, too, but he didn't seem to care a hang. And if the family didn't keep a close watch over him, dear little Johnny would haul whole messes of these herbs home and come close to stuffing the house with them.

He was keen about birds and animals too. He'd rather listen to a wild bird tuning up his pipes—even if the bird was a hoarse old crow—than eat a piece of pumpkin pie with blackberry jam on it. He was never happier than when he was lugging around some little animal or other, even if, say, it was a skunk, an animal many people sort of tried to avoid. And whenever an animal in the neighborhood was sick or had a broken leg, the neighbors would say:

"Take the brute over to Johnny Chapman; he'll fix him up for you."

Any time he got hold of an animal in a fix like that, he'd wrap bandages around scratched places or put splints around broken legs. Or if a dog or cat was sick, he'd feed the beast some of the bad-tasting medicine he'd made out of herbs.

Before long, the animal would perk up and go kiting it

for home, as fast as four legs and a tail would carry it. So it appears that this cure worked pretty well.

When he wasn't doctoring helpless little animals, Johnny would be reading. The book he liked best, for some years, was the one by Aesop, the old Greek slave, that told about animals who kept doing human things—such as lying, cheating, or stealing from one another. Naturally, an animal lover like Johnny was tickled no end by a book that flattered dumb brutes that way.

But in time Johnny's father, a preacher, began to call his attention to the Bible, "There are animals in the Bible, sonny," his father pointed out, "all those animals in the Garden of Eden that were friendly, for instance, and didn't eat one another up, and those animals that took the excursion on Noah's ark, and Balaam's ass, and the four horses of the Apocalypse. Matter of fact, the Bible swarms with animals."

Result was Johnny started to read the Bible for the animals in it. When he found that this book also had a good many parts about apples, that made him think the book was just about perfect. And after a while, when he could catch on to the ideas, they were as much to his taste as the animals and the apples.

They say that Johnny got to be so fond of these two books, *Aesop's Fables* and the Bible, that even after he'd gone to Harvard College and got highly educated, he still couldn't find any books that came within twenty yards of giving him so much pleasure.

It was shortly after Johnny got thoroughly educated that the Chapman family picked up and went to Pittsburgh. And it was in Pittsburgh that something happened to Johnny that made him behave the way he did the rest of his days.

He didn't change, mind you—just got to be more so.

Just what happened isn't clear. Some say that a woman somehow found she couldn't keep her promise to marry Johnny, and that affected him. Some say Johnny got malaria, and it did things to him he didn't get over. Some claim that he got kicked in the head by a horse he was trying to doctor. Still others incline to the idea that it wasn't any of these things, but all three working together. And if all three of these things did happen to him within the space of a short time, you can understand that there'd be likely to be some noticeable results.

Whatever the cause was, Johnny hit on the idea of getting into this business—or "mission," as he called it—of spreading apple trees all over the Middle West.

His idea was that there ought to be more apple trees in the pioneer parts of Pennsylvania and Ohio and Indiana, and he was the fellow to see to it that there were. So each fall, in cider making time, he'd get around to the sweet-smelling cider presses in Pennsylvania. There he'd collect the pomace, the mashed up stuff that was left after the juice had been squoze out of the apples. Then he'd wash the seeds out, and let them dry in the sun. There were only a few things he liked better than rubbing his finger tips over the slick seeds.

The next spring, he'd bag these seeds, some in old coffee sacks or flour sacks, some in little deerskin pouches. Then he'd start tromping westwards, carrying seed packets of one kind and another along with him. He'd hand out the little pouches to the movers West, one to each family. The big bundles he'd tote along to use himself, stopping here and there to plant the seeds all along rivers, in meadows, wherever people would let him or there weren't any people. Even after the seedlings got a good start in some of the orchards, Johnny Appleseed (as he was called by now) would drop around every so often to tend them.

What Johnny would do, in short, was to go traipsing all over the country, sleeping out in the open, eating whatever was handy, stumbling through the trackless forest or tramping through mud and snow, to get these apple orchards started. As the years passed, he covered plenty of ground, too—made it as far south as Tennessee and as far west as the Rocky Mountains.

Some people claimed it was pretty silly.

Maybe you'll ask what people thought was foolish about it. The answer they'd give would be that he wouldn't take any money for going to all this trouble—not a red cent. And it's well known, these people point out, that the only reason that makes sense for doing things is to make money.

"Money?" Johnny Appleseed would say, "*that* for money!" And he'd snap his horny fingers. "I've got a mission, that's what I've got. What do you do with money? Just spend it for clothes or houses or food, I understand, and a saint doesn't care a snippet for any of these. Fact is, he sneers at them, every time he gets a chance. Only thing I want is to get these apples, and herbs that're good for folks, scattered all over the Middle West."

So he'd give those pioneer families appleseeds—free. And if they'd let him have a little ground for his tree nurseries, he'd plant whole orchards for them, and tend the seedlings, too—free. In the course of a few years, he had nurseries all along the shores of Lake Erie, along Elk Creek, Walnut Creek, French Creek, along the Grand River, the Muskingum, the Tuscarawas, the Mohican, and hundreds of other lakes, rivers and creeks. And instead of selling the seedlings from these nurseries (as he easily could have done), he'd heel them in and wrap them in wet straw and give them to the movers*—free.

When anybody brought up the matter of animals, Appleseed was likely to go through that finger-snapping business again. "Leave animals alone," he'd say, "and they'll do the same by you. They're brothers and sisters to you, sort of, only they don't borrow clothes and other truck and they don't misunderstand you the way human brothers and sisters do."

*pioneers.

201

And he'd do the strangest things about varmints you ever heard tell of. One night some of those Ohio mosquitoes came along—some of those pests that are so big that, to set them apart from the common little ones, some people call them gallinippers. Well, Johnny had a fire out there in the woods, and considerable smoke was coming out with the flames. He noticed that these gallinippers kept getting into the smoke and choking to death, or maybe flying into the flames and getting cremated.

At a time like that, most people would just say, "Yaah, serves the brutes right," and chuck more wood on the fire.

But Johnny said, "Poor things! Guess I'll have to put out that fire." Then he sloshed water over the blaze, and lay there shivering in the dark—and being et by gallinippers, the rest of the night.

Then there was the time that Johnny was going to Mansfield to Mt. Vernon one cold winter's day, slushing through the snow in those bark sandals of his. Night came, no cabin was near, and he looked around for some big hollow log to sleep in. He found a dandy, built a fire near by, cooked his mush, slupped the stuff up, and started to crawl into the hollow log.

When he'd got in about to his hips, though, he heard a groaning grunt. Peeking in, helped by the light of the fire, he saw a big bear lying in there with his paws crossed on his chest, enjoying his winter snooze.

Johnny backed out, inch by inch, slow as a snail, being quiet so as not to interrupt the bear's sleep. "Beg your pardon, Brother Bear," he whispered. "I didn't mean to bother your sleep. Saints love bears too much to disturb them any."

Then he yawned, stretched, and curled up in the snow.

People that claimed Johnny was touched said that if all these facts didn't show it, they could mention at least three more. One was that he never ate meat, because of this liking he had for varmints. A second was that he kept planting dog fennel, as well as appleseeds, all over the country. "Dog fennel," he said, "keeps away malaria and typhoid and heaven knows what all." (He was wrong, of course: all it does is smell bad and choke up vegetable gardens.) A third was that though he never exactly came out and said it, he kept hinting all the time that he was a saint.

But some people kept arguing against anybody that tried to run down Johnny Appleseed in any way. "He was a hero and a saint," they'd say. "He had something he believed in, enough to suffer for—and he went to a lot of trouble to bring it about. Talk about overcoming hardships! Why he'd go traipsing around without any shoes, in his bare feet, dressed up in a gunny sack,* in the coldest weather. He didn't even have a decent hat: either he'd wear that pan he cooked mush in or he'd wear that cardboard affair he'd made that looked like a conductor's cap. And why? Simply because he was sweet and good and he wanted to get orchards scattered all over the countryside to look pretty and grow apples for folks."

Well, you can see there are arguments for both sides.

*a coarse jute sack.

Notes on the Stories

"The Giant Sturgeon". From Thomas B. Leekley's *The World of Man-abozho: Tales of the Chippewa Indians* (New York, Vanguard, 1965). Stories of the trickster-hero; this tale reminds the reader of Jonah and the whale.

"How the Seven Brothers Saved Their Sister". From Grace Penney's *Tales of the Cheyenne* (Boston, Houghton Mifflin, 1953). A myth about the constellation called the Pleiades, a transformation story comparable to the Greek myth in which Orion the hunter pursues the seven sisters and Zeus changes them into stars.

"In the Beginning". Retold by Frances Martin in *Raven-Who-Sets-Things-Right: Indian Tales of the Northwest* (New York, Harper & Row, c. 1951; 1975). These are versions recounted by native storytellers "before the tribes had much contact with non-Indian culture". In the far north-west of North America Indians believed that Raven had been the creator of the Sun, Moon, Stars, and Earth. Raven was a shapeshifter and by turns kind and tricky.

"Raven Lets out the Daylight". From the above collection; a North Pacific Coast flood story. The theft of light is recounted in widespread tales.

"How Coyote Brought Fire". From Gail Robinson's and Douglas Hill's *Coyote the Trickster*. (London, Chatto & Windus, 1975; New York, Crane-Russak, 1976). A retelling by two Canadian poets who have spent some time among the Indians. Coyote is one of the most celebrated of all tricksters. The stealing of fire motif appears in many tales, among the Indians and in other lands.

"How Glooskap Found Summer". Retold with slight word changes from Charles Godfrey Leland's *The Algonquin Legends of New England; or Myths and Folk Lore of the Micmac, Passamaquoddy, and Penobscot Tribes* (Boston, Houghton Mifflin, 1884). Leland, a famous early collector in Eastern Canada and Maine, was recognized as the friend and teacher of the Indians, from whom he gathered a store of oral traditions considered to be richer than that of the Chippewa or Iroquois from whom Henry Rowe Schoolcraft collected and recorded. Leland's notes point out the relationships of tales about his culture hero Glooskap with the Norse sagas and Eddas and the legends of the Eskimos.

"Sedna the Sea Goddess". From Helen R. Caswell's retelling in *Shadows from the Singing House* (Rutland, Vermont, Charles Tuttle, 1968). This most famous Eskimo creation myth has a typical stark quality and the supernatural characteristically plays an important role. Sedna, the mother of sea animals, is the great culture heroine of the Eskimos.

"How Saynday Got the Sun". A Kiowa Indian tale about the culture hero Saynday, from *Winter-telling Stories* by Alice Marriott (New York, Crowell, c. 1947; 1969). Told by a trained ethnologist who became a specialist on the arts and crafts of many Indian tribes and a student particularly of the life of those of the Great Central Plains. Saynday is the trickster hero of stories that always begin "Saynday was coming along. . . ."

"Big Long Man's Corn Patch". From Dorothy Hogner's *Navajo Winter Nights* (New York, Nelson, 1935). A story found with others when the compiler and her artist husband visited the Navajo Reservation in Arizona and New Mexico. Like James Mooney's "The Rabbit and the Tar Wolf" in his *Myths of the Cherokee* (U.S. Bureau of American Ethnology. Nineteenth Annual Report, 1897–8), this is closely related to the African-American tar-baby tale of the south-east.

"Poor Turkey Girl". Retold by the compiler of this volume from the version in Frank H. Cushing's *Zuñi Folk Tales* (New York, Knopf, 1936). One of a number of Indian Cinderella tales, this one clearly shows its relationships to European tales, but has a distinctly different, unhappy ending.

"The Indian Cinderella". From Cyrus Macmillan's *Canadian Wonder Tales* (London, New York, John Lane, 1918) and *Glooskap's Country and Other Indian Tales* (Toronto, New York, Oxford University Press, 1956, which includes also Macmillan's *Canadian Fairy Tales* of 1922, the combined volume today being published by the Bodley Head, 1974). Glooskap, who figures in these tales, is the Eastern Canadian counterpart of Manabozho or Nanabozho (Hiawatha), one who has been compared to Hercules as the performer of miracles and daring deeds.

"Star Maiden". Retold by this anthologist from Henry Rowe Schoolcraft's early telling of Indian legends in *Algic Researches* (1839). The hero Waupee is one of a number of Indian heroes whose trials are recounted by Schoolcraft. The motif of descent from or ascent to the heavens is a distinctive Indian mythological element.

"Scarface; or, a California-Prairie Tale". From George B. Grinnell's *Blackfeet Indian Stories* (New York, Scribner, 1913: stories from *Black-*

foot Lodge Tales; the Story of a Prairie People, Scribner, 1892 [University of Nebraska Press, 1962, paper]). Grinnell, a distinguished early ethnologist, presented his tales in a succession of editions. Scarface is a favorite Indian hero with child readers.

"The Blessed Gift of Joy Is Bestowed Upon Man" ("Ermine Is Carried Off by the Young Eagle"). From Knud Rasmussen's *The Eagle's Gift; Alaskan Eskimo Tales* (New York, Doubleday, 1952) as translated by Isobel Hutchinson. One of the most delightful tales collected by this Danish expedition leader in Arctic America 1921–4. Rasmussen considered it his great fortune to have been translated thus.

"The Tar Baby". (Water-Well Version). From Dora Lee Newman's *Marion County in the Making* (Fairmont, Marion County, West Virginia, 1918). A Black American tale deriving clearly from African lore, incorporating such animals as the elephant, monkey, and giraffe. Its story line parallels in many details Joel Chandler Harris's famous story "The Wonderful Tar-baby", but is told without the heavy colloquialisms.

"How Ole Woodpecker Got Ole Rabbit's Conjure Bag". From Mary Alicia Owen's *Old Rabbit the Voodoo and Other Sorcerers* (London, T. Fisher Unwin, 1893). Edited for this volume with minimal word change. An introduction by Charles Godfrey Leland describes the existence in Missouri, as "all along the Border", of a mixed race of Blacks and Indian descent who have "blended their vast stock of traditions"—sorcery, magic, and medicine. In the Owen book, the tales are relayed as told by "old aunties" to a white child, in the manner of the Brer Rabbit stories set down by Joel Chandler Harris.

"The Conjure Wives". Set down by Frances G. Wickes in *Holiday Stories* (Chicago, Rand McNally, 1921) as an old southern tale. "Conjurer" (man or woman) means a practitioner of magic or witchcraft.

"Wiley and the Hairy Man". Another tale of conjury, slightly edited here from Donnell Van de Voort's version for the Federal Writers Project of the Works Project Administration for the State of Alabama.

"Jean Sotte". Set down by folklorist Alcée Fortier in *Louisiana Folk-Tales in French Dialect and English* (published for the Folklore Society by Houghton Mifflin, 1895). A world-wide numbskull type of tale, this is one of many stories found by this university professor in Louisiana, who devoted years to the collecting and preparation of these tales for publication. A number of them appeared first in the *Journal of American Folklore*.

"How Jack Went to Seek his Fortune". A version given by Francis L. Palmer in the *Journal of American Folklore* (v. 1, 1888: 227–28). Contributed by a New Englander, this is one of a cluster of "English folk-tales in America" in the first volume of this journal.

'The Twist-mouth Family". A Kentucky story which appeared in the *Journal of American Folklore* (v. 18, 1905: 322–23). For maximum humor, this tale should be heard from a storyteller with a mobile mouth. Folklorist Maria Leach, who included it in her *Rainbow Book of American Folklore* (Cleveland, World, 1958), reported hearing it first from a Nova Scotian in New York and thus concluded that it came from the British Isles, but recognized that it belonged also to Kentucky. Stith Thompson cites a Danish source as well.

"A Stepchild that was treated mighty Bad". From Marie Campbell's *Tales from the Cloud-Walking Country* (Bloomington, Indiana University Press, 1960). Collected by a teacher in the southern mountains who found ballads and tales traceable "across the ocean waters clear back to the old country".

"Nippy and the Yankee Doodle". In Leonard Roberts's *Old Greasybeard; Tales from the Cumberland Gap* (Detroit Folklore Associates, 1969; earlier published in *Nippy and the Yankee Doodle and More Folk Tales from the Southern Mountains* (Berea, Kentucky, The Council of the Southern Mountains, 1958). Roberts, a college teacher and native of Kentucky, collected these tales, still current in an active oral tradition of the Appalachian South, from informants known to his students. This story is clearly related to Joseph Jacobs' English "Molly Whuppie".

"Old Fire Dragaman". From Richard Chase's *Jack Tales* (Boston, Houghton Mifflin, 1943), a collection gathered by this storyteller in Southern Appalachia from informants in an isolated pocket. It is clearly related to Joseph Jacobs' stories and many European folk tales, Jack being the counterpart of Boots or Cinderlad, a kind of culture hero or trickster. Chase, adopting the mountain locale and speech, describes his Appalachian giant-killer as having "easy-going, unpretentious rural American manners". His sub-title for the *Jack Tales* is "Told by R. M. Ward and his kindred in the Beech Mountain section of Western North Carolina and by other descendants of Council Harmon (1803–96) elsewhere in the Southern Mountains; with three tales from Wise County, Virginia."

"Pecos Bill becomes a Coyote". From James Cloyd Bowman's *Pecos Bill, the Greatest Cowboy of All Time* (Chicago, Albert Whitman, 1937). The hobbyist-folklorist collected from many sources: storytellers at campfire and round-up and original documents about the unexplored West where "individualism" in the frontiersman flourished to the point where, he says, men began to exaggerate for amusement. Freeing themselves from the hard and cruel world, thus they created Pecos Bill. "One tall tale naturally led to a taller tale. Accounts showed that Bill, lost out of his parents' covered wagon somewhere near the Pecos River when he was a baby, was adopted by the coyote and lived with them for years, until he was discovered and persuaded to become a cowboy and accomplished astounding feats on his horse Widow Maker."

"Babe the Blue Ox". From Esther Shephard's *Paul Bunyan* (New York, Harcourt Brace Jovanovich, 1924). An epic sequence of stories grew up about this "mythical hero of the woods, a kind of super lumberjack", noted for his cleverness. The version here comes from one of the fuller accounts for young people. Tales about Paul Bunyan are thought to have originated among loggers of Quebec or Northern Ontario, "who may have brought them from the old country". They are known to have carried them from the east, via Minnesota, where they were influenced by Scandinavian stories, and thence to the Northwest.

"Stormalong Fights the Kraken". From Anne B. Malcolmson's and Dell McCormick's *Old Stormalong* (Boston, Houghton, 1952). A giant seaman from Boston, Massachusetts, Old Stormalong sailed all over the world performing outsize feats of strength and ingenuity.

"Strong but Quirky". A chapter from Irwin Shapiro's *Yankee Thunder; the Legendary Life of Davy Crockett* (New York, Messner, 1944). Like Daniel Boone, Davy Crockett was a popular frontiersman of history about whom many legends came to be told, both pure fact and folklore.

"Johnny Appleseed". From Walter Blair's *Tall Tale America, a Legendary History of Our Humorous Heroes* (New York, Coward, McCann, Geoghegan, 1944). A chapter from Professor Blair's standard anthology of tall-tale literature prepared for young people. This describes the wanderings of the New Englander Jonathan Chapman through the wilderness, casting appleseeds as he went and becoming a friend of the Indians.

Some Suggestions for Further Reading

General

Botkin, Benjamin A., ed. *A Treasury of American Folklore: Stories, Ballads, and Traditions of the People*. New York, Crown, 1944.

Dorson, Richard M. *American Folklore*. Chicago, University of Chicago, 1959.

Emrich, Duncan. *The Hodgepodge Book; an Almanac of American Folklore*. Illus. by Ib Ohlsson. New York, Four Winds, 1972. One of several amusing collections gathered for children by this folklorist.

Leach, Maria. *The Rainbow Book of American Folk Tales*. Illus. by Marc Simont. New York, Crowell, 1958. An anthology for young people.

Indian and Eskimo

Ayre, Robert. *Sketko, the Raven*. Illus. by Philip Survey. Toronto, Macmillan 1967. Paper, Scholastic Book Service, 1974.

Curry, Jane Louise. *Down from the Lonely Mountain; California Indian Tales*. Illus. by Enrico Arno. New York, Harcourt Brace Jovanovich, 1964. A dozen tales of the world when it was young.

Field, Edward. *Eskimo Songs and Stories*. Collected by Knud Rasmussen on the Fifth Thule Expedition. Illus. Kiakshuk and Pudlo. New York, Delacorte/Seymour Lawrence, 1973. Brief, free-verse translations.

Fisher, Anne B. *Stories California Indians Told*. Illus. by Ruth Robbins. Berkeley, California, Parnassus Press, 1957. Of Coyote and the gaining of light, fire, and mountains.

Gillham, Charles E. *Beyond the Clapping Mountains: Eskimo Stories from Alaska*. Illus. by Chanimum. New York, Macmillan, 1945. Thirteen animal folk tales gathered from an English-speaking Eskimo and illustrated by an Eskimo artist.

Harris, Christie. *Once Upon a Totem*. Illus. by John Frazer Mills. New York, Atheneum, 1963. Legends of the West Coast Indians.

Hayes, William D. *Indian Tales of the Desert People*. Illus. by the reteller. New York, McKay, 1957.

Highwater, Jamake. *Anpao: An American Indian Odyssey*. Illustrated by Fritz Scholder. Philadelphia, Lippincott. 1977. A full-length hero tale about Anpao-Scarface, son of the Sun, and his quest to lose his

211

scar and win the beautiful Ko-ko-mik-e-is. Into the poetic narration of this famous legend is woven other Indian lore, about the creation, dread encounters, and magic feats. The artist and the teller are both Indian.

Hill, Kay. *Badger the Mischief Maker*. Illus. by John Hamberger. New York, Dodd, Mead, 1965. Tales about the trickster in Glooskap's world in Eastern Canada. Also, *Glooskap and His Magic*.

Hodges, Margaret. *The Fire Bringer: a Paiute Indian Legend*. Illus. by Peter Parnall. Boston, Little, 1972. An attractive adaptation from Mary Austin's version in *Basket Woman* of 1904.

Houston, James. *Tikta'liktak; an Eskimo Legend*. Illus. by the reteller. New York, Harcourt Brace Jovanovich, 1965. An Arctic survival tale.

—— *The White Archer; an Eskimo Legend*. Ibid., 1967.

Marriott, Alice Lee, and Carol K. Rachlin. *Plains Indian Mythology*. New York, Crowell, 1976. Myths, legends, and contemporary lore representing many tribes; one of many books by these specialists, for older readers.

Martin, Frances. *Nine Tales of Coyote*. Illus. By Dorothy McIntee. New York, Harper and Row, 1950.

Melzack, Ronald. *The Day Tuk Became a Hunter and Other Eskimo Tales*. Illus. by Carol Jones. New York, Dodd, Mead, 1968.

Reid, Dorothy, M. *Tales of Nanabozho*. Illus. by Donald Grant. Toronto, Oxford University Press, 1963: London, 1964; New York, David McKay, 1963. The creator-magician of the Ojibwa (the Hiawatha of Longfellow's poem).

Thompson, Stith. *European Tales Among the North American Indians*. Colorado Springs, Colorado, Colorado College, 1919. Of interest to adults.

—— *Tales of the North American Indians*. Cambridge, Massachusetts, Harvard University Press, 1929; reprint, Bloomington, Indiana, Indiana University Press, 1966. Of interest to adults.

Black American

Courlander, Harold. *Terrapin's Pot of Sense*. Illus. by Elton Fax. New York, Holt, Rinehart, and Winston, 1957. Humorous animal tales clearly related to the African.

—— *A Treasury of Afro-American Folklore*. New York, Crown, 1976. An adult source.

Dorson, Richard M. *American Negro Folktales*. New York, Fawcett, 1968. Studies for adults.

Faulkner, William J. *The Days When the Animals Talked; Black American Folktales and How They Came To Be*. Illustrated by Troy Howell. Chicago, Follet. 1977. Tales heard by the compiler as a boy at the turn of the century from an elderly ex-slave. The narratives, set down in standard English, include folk reminiscences of plantation injustices and frustrations, and stories resembling the Uncle Remus tales, about the trickster Brer Rabbit; both types are protest tales exemplifying the conflict between the strong and the weak.

Harris, Joel Chandler. *The Complete Tales of Uncle Remus*. Compiled by Richard Chase. Illus. By A. B. Frost and others. Boston, Houghton Mifflin, 1955. Stories arranged in order of publication, from the numerous collections made by Harris. All of the stories with their heavy dialect present problems for editors and for young readers.

Lester, Julius. *The Knee-High Man and Other Tales*. Illus. by Jack Pinto. New York, Dial, 1972. Tales heard by the teller in his childhood. For younger readers.

Parsons, Elsie Clews. *Folk-lore of the Sea Islands, South Carolina*. Cambridge, Massachusetts, Metro Books, 1923. Reprint 1969. Gullah tales recorded in their black dialect, as collected by a well known folklorist, for adults.

European Tales Brought by Immigrants

Barbeau, Charles Marius. *The Golden Phoenix, and Other French-Canadian Fairy Tales*. Illus. by Arthur Price. New York, Walck, 1958.

Bell, Corydon. *John Rattling-Gourd of Big Cove*. New York, Macmillan, 1955. Appalachian stories.

Carlson, Natalie Savage. *The Talking Cat, and Other Stories of French Canada*. Illus. by Roger Duvoisin. New York, Harper and Row, 1952. Chatty, hearsay stories of the folk.

Chase, Richard. *Grandfather Tales: American-English Folk Tales*. Boston, Houghton Mifflin, 1948. A companion to his 1943 *Jack Tales*.

Jagendorf, Moritz A. *The New England Bean-Pot; American Folk Stories To Read and To Tell*. Illus. by Donald McKay. New York, Vanguard, 1948.

———— *Sand in the Bag and Other Folk Stories of Ohio, Indiana, and Illinois*. Illus. by Jack Moment. New York, Vanguard, 1952.

———— *Upstate, Downstate; Folk Stories of the Middle Atlantic States*. Illus. by Howard Simon. New York, Vanguard, 1949.

Tall Tales

Bowman, James C. *Mike Fink*. Illus. by Leonard Everett Fisher. Boston, Little, Brown, 1957. A companion to this teller's *Pecos Bill*, this describes the exploits of the legendary riverman.

Carmer, Carl. *The Hurricane's Children*. New York, McKay, 1967. Many tall-tale narratives are included here.

Daugherty, James. *Daniel Boone*, with original lithographs in color by the author. New York, Viking, 1939.

SOME SUGGESTIONS FOR FURTHER READING

Felton, Harold W. *Pecos Bill, Texas Cowpuncher*. Illus. by Aldren Watson. New York, Knopf, 1949. Felton has dealt in other volumes with Bowleg Bill (seagoing cowpuncher), John Henry, and Paul Bunyan.

Hunt, Mabel Leigh. *Better Known as Johnny Appleseed*. Illus. by James Daughtery. Philadelphia, Lippincott, 1950. A full treatment, as fictionalized biography.

Malcolmson, Anne B., *and* Dell J. McCormick. *Mister Stormalong*. Illus. by Joshua Tolford. Boston, Houghton Mifflin, 1952. A colorful full-length account. Her *Yankee Doodle's Cousins* presents short tales about twenty-eight heroes.

Rounds, Glen. *Ol' Paul, the Mighty Logger*. Illus. by the reteller. New York, Holiday, 1949. Humorous narration, fully illustrated for younger readers.

Rourke, Constance. *Davy Crockett*. New York, Harcourt Brace Jovanovich, 1934. A biography balancing the historical and legendary hero.

Schwartz, Alvin. *Whoppers: Tall Tales and Other Lies Collected from American Folklore*. Illus. by Glen Rounds. Philadelphia, Lippincott, 1975. Folksy humorous anecdotes, for younger readers.

Stevens, James. *Paul Bunyan*. New York, Knopf, 1947.